ALL WRAPPED UP

DH Books published by
DH Publishing Company
P.O. Box 333
Indianapolis, IN 46250

ISBN: 978-1-73365028-1
Book cover Design: DH Publishing Company
Publisher DH Publishing Company
www.DHpublishingco.com

Printed in the United States of America

DH Books

Table of Contents

ACKNOWNLEGDEMENT

Wow! God, I just want to thank you for another book and another opportunity to work with more talented people. I would like to thank my support system my son Daniel Powell and my daughter Devin Hill and all of my readers. I hope you enjoy this book for the holidays.
Denise Hill

Giving honor to God without whom I am nothing. I want to acknowledge my family for their love and support Olon, Jalen, Jordyn, Jessica and my father, Larry for being the biggest blessings. Special acknowledgement and birthday wish to my grandmother Roberta. I'd also like to thank DH Publishing for opening its doors to me. I'm looking forward to even greater opportunities in the future and praying for the company's continued success!
Cereda Smith

I started the new year out with the goal of writing a book, but by God's grace this is my second one this year. I want to thank my family, and friends, for their support &

encouragement. You never know what you can do if you don't try.

Dwuna Henton

The Christmas List

CHAPTER 1

Sitting at the kitchen table, Tamara sat with a big smile plastered across her face as a tall, caramel color handsome man danced across her living room floor, removing each piece of clothing one by one as he danced to the sound of Ginuwine's, 'Pony'.

"Yeah, baby, take it all off," Tamara yelled.

When he got to his pants, he slowly unzipped his zipper as the sound of two young teenagers' voices filled the room.

"Mom! Mom! Her twin daughters yelled out to her.

"Are you daydreaming again," Drake asked, the younger twin by two minutes.

Her daughters' voices pulled her from her daze.

"No, I wasn't daydreaming again. I was simply thinking out loud."

"What were you thinking about?" The older twin Blake asked.

"Yeah, who were you yelling to take it all off?" Drake chimed in.

The girls laughed as they teased their mom

"Take it off, take it all off," Drake said

"No one. You two wouldn't understand," Tamara said as she blushed from embarrassment.

"Try us."

"If you two don't get out of here and get ready for bed."

Upstairs in their bedroom. The girls were planning to set their mom up with their substitute teacher.

"It has to work since tomorrow is his last day as our teacher," Blake said.

"I know."

But what if it doesn't work?" Drake asked.

"It has too," Her sister said.

The next day, the teenagers were so excited. They knew Mr. Clarke, the substitute teacher, and their mom would make a perfect couple.

Blake and Drake couldn't wait for their six-period class.

The bell rang for the sixth period. The two sisters rushed down the hall to their class.

As they walked in, he stood at six feet two inches tall, nice build, half black half Puerto Rican with his jet black wavy hair. He looked like he had just stepped off the cover of a magazine. He was the spitting image of Shawn Clark on the television series Single Ladies."

Blake just stood and admired while Drake walked over to Mr. Stanley Clarke.

"Hey Mr. Clarke, how are you?

Mr. Clarke looked up to see Drake standing in front of his desk.

"Well, hello, Drake. I'm good and thanks for asking. How are you?"

"I'm good, but I would be even better if you would accept my mom's invite to be a guest on her radio show to talk about your publishing business. Then you could talk with her about publishing her novel."

"Oh, so she wants me to be a guest on her radio show?"

"Yep, she sure does," Blake said as she walked up.

"That's sounds awesome." He reached into his jacket pocket and pulled out a business card. "Give this to your mom and have her call me so we can set up a time to meet."

"Thanks, Mr. Clarke, you won't regret it."

Later that evening, when they sat at the

dinner table, the girls began whispering back and forth.

"Okay, that's enough. What is all the whispering for?"

"You tell her," Blake said.

"Mom, remember us telling you about our substitute teacher and how he helps people publish their books?"

"Vaguely, why?"

"He wants to be on your radio show to talk about his publishing business and then talk with you about publishing your novel," Drake said.

"Really, he wants to help me publish my novel?"

"Yep."

Drake handed her mom his business card.

"Here, you can call him now and set up a meeting."

"I will not. I will call him in the morning on my first break."

Later that night, Tamara sat in bed excited and nervous at the same time. She had been putting off finishing her romance novel, but now she has a reason to finish it. "But what if he doesn't like it?" She asked herself. When Tamara finally laid her head down on her pillows, she turned to the side and smiled. She stared as he removed his shirt.

"I've been waiting for this all day. But we have to make sure the girls don't hear us," She said as she allowed him to remove her nightshirt exposing her voluptuous breast and thighs as Al Green's 'Tired of Being Alone' played in the background.

He crawled between her legs, and his tongue found her breasts. He let his tongue caress her nipple until it became hard, and then he wrapped his soft lips around it.

"Oh baby, you are making me so hot right nos," Tamara whispered, trying to keep her voice down.

"You ain't felt nothing yet." He began to move down south kissing every inch of her body until he found her treasure.

"Are you ready for me, baby?" He asked, and right before she could answer, her alarm on her phone went off.

Tamara sat up, looked around the room before she reached over, grabbed her phone off the nightstand, and turned it off. She sat up in bed in disarray. She glanced around the room again.

"What the fuck!"

Tamara had been dreaming about the mystery man again.

"Nah, this has got to stop, but it felt so real. This man got me all horny and shit," She said as she made her way into the bathroom to take a shower.

That afternoon, Tamara sat behind her desk at the radio station on lunch break. After eating her lunch, she laid her head down on her desk as she began to dream. There he was, standing at the counter paying for his purchases. Tamara stood there in awe. He slowly walked toward her. She couldn't move, she froze in her tracks, and as he walked past her, he gave her a smile that melted her heart.

"Oh my God!" Tamara said as she turned to watch as he walked out of the store. Tamara watched him until he was out of her sight.

"Tamara, Tamara," her co-host said as he nudged her.

Tamara raised her head to see Thomas standing over her. Thomas, an African American ex-football player, stood at six feet three inches tall. He was built like a quarterback with eyes the color of honey and his Hershey's chocolate skin, who resembled Harold House Moore, but older, greeted her.

She smiled at him as she asked him, "What are you doing?"

"Girl, we have two minutes until we are back on the air.
How did you fall asleep so quickly?"

"Oh my God!" She said as she stood up, rushed out of the breakroom, and walked down the hall beside him. "I didn't sleep well last night," She said.

"Why, did that man keep you up too late?"
Tamara looked like a deer caught in headlights.

"What man!"

"Whoa, calm down. I was only playing." Tamara laughed as she sat down and put her headphones on.
Thomas and Tamara have been co-hosting the morning and afternoon show for over five years now. Even though he has had a crush on her for the last three years. Thomas had never come on to her, he treated her like one of his homeboys. The first time Tamara laid eyes on him, she was very much attracted to him. But as time went by, she realized the attraction was one-sided. He became more like a big brother to her.

"You're on the air with Tarmar Reynolds and Thomas Jackson on Love in the Afternoon. How's everyone doing on this cold and dreary afternoon. I hope everyone has that special someone to go home to this evening and cuddle up to. I wish I had someone. You know what, I'm going to put a man on my Christmas list."

"Your Christmas list?"

"Yes, you heard me right, my Christmas list. You know how the kids make a Christmas list for Santa. I'm going to make one for Santa. How many of you listeners out there make a Christmas list for Santa? Give us a call at 515-231-9087 and tell us what you have on your Christmas list."

Three hours later, Tamara and Thomas ended their radio show.

"What are you getting ready to do?" Tamara asked.

"I'm getting ready to call this little honey, I met at the club last week."
Tamara shook her head. "You are something else," She said as she walked off. Little did she know he had nowhere to go just like she didn't.

CHAPTER 2

Later that night, Tamara finally decided to call Mr. Stanley Clarke. She sat in bed and slowly dialed his number. Tamara couldn't understand why she was so nervous. It wasn't like she was trying to date him. As Tamara continued to think, the smooth sound of Stanley Clarke's voice echoed through the phone.

"Hello... Hello!"

"I'm sorry, can I speak with Mr. Clarke?"

"This is Mr. Clarke."

The sound of his voice made her body tingle all over.

"Hi, this is Tamara Reynolds. Drake and Blake Reynolds, mom."

"Okay, how are you?"

Tamara pulled at the covers because his voice sounded so good. She could just picture him.

"Are you there?"

"Yes, I'm here. I'm good and you?

"Oh, I can't complain."

"I bet." She said before she knew what she had said.

"I was calling to see when would be a

good time for us to meet. Maybe we can have dinner, lunch, or maybe coffee."

"We could do coffee Saturday morning," Mr. Clarke said. "How does Starbucks sound? Let's say around 10 am on E 96th street?"

"Great! I'll see you then," Tamara said.
That night, Tamara had another dream about the mystery man. But this time, she had a voice to go with his face. It was the voice of Stanley Clarke.
And this time, he was joining her in the shower. Tamara smiled once she saw his naked body enter the bathroom.
She stood there as she took him all in.

"Damn, baby. You look so good. Bring yo fine ass over here," she said as she grabbed hold of his arm and pulled him to her. She reached up and pulled his head down so she could get a feel of his soft lips on hers.

"How bad do you want this?" He asked as he began to kiss her. He moved to her neck and then her breasts.

"I want you so bad," She said.

"I don't believe you. Make me believe it."

"I want you so damn bad." She grabbed

18

hold of him and started rubbing him until he became long and hard, and then she rubbed him against her clit. Tamara slowly inserted him inside.

"Oh, Stanley!" She screamed so loud that she had awakened herself out of her dream.

Tamara laid there for a minute before turning on her bedroom light. Her nightshirt was drenched.

"What in the hell is going on with me?" She whispered to herself.

Three hours later, Tamara's alarm on her phone went off, she was tired. She thought about calling off, but she had never called off, and she didn't want to start now.

At work, when she walked into the break room, everyone turned to look at her. She was always chipper and outgoing, but this morning she was quiet as a church mouse.

"Hey, is everything okay?" Thomas asked as Tamara poured herself a cup of coffee.

"I'm good. I'm just tired. I haven't been sleeping so good, and it's getting to me."

"Do you need big daddy to rock you to sleep?"

Tamara gave him an evil look and rolled her eyes.

Thomas burst out laughing. "You know I tickle myself sometimes."

"I don't know why... it ain't like you funny!"

"That ain't what the ladies say."

"Well, they're probably just stupid." She said as she walked away.

"Man, you are grumpy."

After the morning show, Tamara went into her manager's office and laid across her couch. She set the alarm on her phone for five minutes before the afternoon show.

Stanley Clarke sat in his recliner as he waited for the afternoon radio show with Tamara Reynolds. He couldn't get her voice out of his head. Her voice was so soothing. He could listen to her talk all day. He couldn't wait to see if her voice matched her face, and if it did, he knew he would be in trouble. There was something about Tamara that drew him to her, but he couldn't put his finger on it. He had never met her. He only had the once short conversation with her.

"Welcome to the afternoon show. I'm Tamara Reynolds."

Stanley heard her voice, and he smiled. Stanley got up from the chair and walked over to the window, and stared out.

"Ms. Tamara Reynolds. What is it about you that pulls at me?"

"We had so many calls yesterday from women about their Christmas list," Thomas said.

"I know. I was shocked," Tamara replied.

"So tell me, Tamara, what all did you put on your Christmas list?"

"I have only one item on my list, and that is a man."

Stanley's smile widened, "So, you put a man on your Christmas list."

"I want to know more about you, Ms. Reynolds," Stanley said.

Stanley walked over to his desk. He sat down and turned on his laptop, and got on Facebook. He typed in Tamara Reynold and waited for the results. Several Tamara Reynolds came up. He continued to scroll down and came to a profile picture with a beautiful woman and two twin girls.

Stanley sat there with a smile on his face as he looked at her picture. But still, he wanted to know more about her.

Saturday morning rolled around, and Tamara was trying to find the perfect outfit for her meeting with Mr. Clarke.

She tried on three outfits and still wasn't satisfied.

"Blake and Drake. Can you come in here and help me pick out an outfit to wear?"

Drake walked in. "Just wear anything. It's not like you're going out on a date."

"Where are you going?" Blake asked.

Tamara looked at the girls, "To meet Mr. Clarke."

"You mean our teacher, Mr. Clarke?" She asked excitedly.

"Yes, who else would it be?"

"Well, you need to wear something pretty," Drake said.

Blake looked through her mother's closet.

"Here, wear this. I've always liked you in this, and besides, this color makes your skin tone pop."

Tamara looked at Blake, "Skin tone pop? This is not a date. It's a meeting over a cup of coffee."

"Well, once you see Mr. Clarke, you're gonna wish you would have worn this," Drake said.

"Is that so?"

"Mom, do you know who he reminds me of?" Blake asked.

"No, but I'm sure you're going to tell me."

"You know that guy that played in a few episodes of Soul Food who had a crush on Bird. I think she had an affair with him."

Tamara stood still. She hadn't put two and two together. The mystery man in her dreams was the guy from Soul Food and Single ladies, Terrell Tilford.

"Please, he doesn't look like him," Tamara said.

"You're right. We're just playing," Blake said as she nudged her sister.

Mr. Clarke pulled into the parking lot of Starbucks at 9:50. He was always early, but today, he didn't want to be too early. He sat outside in his pearly white Lexus and waited. Five minutes later, his phone rang.

"Hello."

"Hey, Mr. Clarke, this is Tamara Reynolds. I just pulled into the parking lot. Are you already inside?"

"No, I am outside in my car. What kind of car are you in?"

"I'm in a white pathfinder."

Stanley got out of his car, still on the phone. Four seconds later, he stood at Tarmar's driver's window.

Tamara turned to look and almost passed out. Her mystery man was standing at her window.

"Are you just going to stand there and look, or are you going to get out?"
Stanley laughed. He didn't think Tamara was expecting someone like him.
Tamara finally came to her senses and opened the door, and got out.

"I'm sorry, you just caught me off guard."

"No worries. It happens all the time," Stanley said.

"It's a pleasure to meet you," Stanley said as he hugged Tamara.

"I'm sorry, but I'm a hugger."

"Nice to meet you as well," Tamara said as she got a whiff of his cologne.

"I hope you don't mind me saying so, but you smell hella good."
Stanley laughed. "Thank you."
Inside, Stanley ordered coffee while Tamara got a table.
Stanley walked over and handed Tamara a cup of coffee, and took a seat.

"Thank you."

"So, why do you want to be on my radio show?" Tamara asked.
Stanley smiled. "Wow! Your daughters told

me that you wanted to interview me."

"Really. So did you tell my girls you wanted to help me with publishing my book?"

"No, they told me that you wanted me to publish your novel."

"Those sneaky little girls."
They both laughed.

"I think we have just been set up," Tamara said.

"I ain't mad," Stanley said as he gave Tamara a pretty smile.

"Well, I have to say I ain't mad either."

"You know I listened to your afternoon show yesterday. I like that you made a Christmas list. I might make me a Christmas list," He said as he licked his lips.

"Oh no! Tamara was embarrassed.

"Tell me more about yourself," Stanley said.

"What do you want to know?"

"Why is a beautiful woman like you single?"

"I haven't met the right person, I guess."

"Are you single?" Tamara asked.

"Very much so."

"Why?"

"I guess like you. I haven't met the right person."

"Would you go to dinner with me this evening so I can get to know you a little better?"

"I would love to," Tamara said.

CHAPTER 3

"**M**an, I don't know what to wear!" Tamara screamed.

Blake and Drake sat downstairs watching TV when they heard the mother scream.

"Mom, what's wrong?" The girls asked as they dashed upstairs to her bedroom.

The girls stood at the door, "What's wrong?" Blake asked.

"Nothing, just thinking out loud again."

"You do that quite often, you know," Blake said.

"I know. I have to work on that."

Drake walked inside her mom's room and walked over to the closet. She pulled out this black fitted dress.

"Mom, this is it." She said as she held the dress up.

"Oh my God! That's hot!" Blake shouted.

Stanley stood in the mirror as he dabbed a little of Giorgio Armani on. He turned sideways to see how his new shirt looked with his slacks.

"I hope I'm not overdressed," He said to himself.

Twenty-five minutes later, Stanley pulled into the driveway of Tamara's condo.

Once at the front door, he knocked once, and the girls excitedly jerked the door open.

"Hey Mr. Clarke," the girls yelled.

Stanley laughed at the girl's excitement.

"Ooh we, roses," Blake said.

"Yes, they're for your mom."

"I'll take them and put them in some water," Drake said as her mom walked down the stairs.

"Mom, look at the pretty roses Mr. Clarke bought you."

"Thank you," Tamara said as she stood in the doorway.

"Beautiful roses for a beautiful woman."

"You're so kind."

Thirty minutes later, They pulled into the parking lot of Ruth's Chris on 86th street.

The parking lot was full.

"Wow! I guess everyone had the same idea this evening," Stanley said.

"Right."

Stanley turned off the ignition, got out and walked around to the passenger side, and opened the door for Tamara.

"You know, for it to be November, it feels pretty good out. Would you like to eat out on the terrace with the fire pit or inside?"

"I have to agree. It does feel pretty good out, so let's eat out on the terrace."

Once they were seated, the waiter took their order. They both ordered the King Salmon filet with Roasted Brussel Sprouts, and Fire Roasted Corn.

"Oh my God! Everything looks and smells delicious," Tamara said.

"This is my favorite," Stanley said.

"Really. How often do you come here?"

Stanley laughed. "Every Friday."

"Oh, so that's why they know you by name." Tamara smiled.

"Yeah, pretty much. Do you eat out often?"

"Not really. I prefer to cook. I love cooking."

"Are you any good?"

"Am I any good? My food is so good it will make you wanna slap your momma."

They both laughed.

"Oh, okay. So when are you going to let me find out?"

"How about tomorrow? The girls will be with their dad so it will be just the two of us."

"Just tell me what time and I will be there with bells and whistles on."

Tamara laughed, "You are so crazy."

Once they finished dinner. The waiter brought out a bottle of Penfolds Cabernet Shiraz, Grange from South Australia.

"I guess this is your favorite as well?" Tamara asked as the waiter filled her wine glass.

"Yep. I hope you don't mind me ordering for you?"

"I'll let it slide this time," Tamara said as she smiled.

Thomas met with Sherry, Tamara's best friend. They met at Panara on East 56th street for dinner.

"So how are things at the radio station?" Sherry asked.

Thomas was hesitant to speak.

"Well, and this is just between us two. I haven't told Tamara yet, but I have accepted an offer at another radio station."

"Wow! How do you think she is going to react?"

"She knows what I have been trying to get the station to do, but they refuse to listen. But my new job is giving me full creative control."

"That's good to hear. So now you have nothing standing in your way of pursuing Tamara."

Thomas laughed. "You would say something like that."

"Well, it's the truth. When do you start?"

"In two weeks."

The next day, Tamara had just taken her cornbread out of the oven when she heard a knock at her front door.

Tamara removed her apron and looked herself over in the mirror before answering the door.

"Good afternoon," Stanley said.

"Hey, how are you?" Tamara asked.

"I'm better now that I see your beautiful smile," Stanley said as he handed her a bottle of Peach Moscato wine.

Tamara looked at the bottle, "Oh, one of my favorites."

Tamara and Stanley sat down at the dinner table.

"This looks and smells delicious," Stanley said as he picked up a piece of rib and bit a piece of it.

"Damn! You're right, this tastes so good it does make me want to slap my momma!"

Tamara laughed, "See I told you I could throw down."

"Please, you did more than throw down, baby girl," He said as he put a spoon full of Mac and cheese in his mouth.

31

After dinner, the two sat by the fireplace and talked.

"If you don't mind me asking, how long have you been divorced?"

"I've never been married. The girl's dad and I had been together for two years before I got pregnant, and when that happened, he left. I had no contact with him until about five years ago."

"I'm sorry you had to go through your pregnancy without him."

Tamara smiled. "It was hard, but I have a great support system. My family and friends were there for us."

"That's good to know."

"What about you?"

"I was engaged two years ago, but I called it off when I caught her in bed with her ex."

"I'm sorry to hear that."

"Don't be. If that hadn't happened, I wouldn't be here." Stanley said as he grabbed hold of her hand.

"So true. You know what, I have a confession to make."

Stanley moved closer.

"I had dreams of you before I met you, and I wondered who this man was that kept interrupting my dreams and thoughts."

"Stop pulling my leg."

"I am dead serious."

"Did I do this to you in your dreams?" He asked as he pulled her close to him. He brushed his lips against hers. She opened her mouth to allow him to enter.

The kiss made her toes curl. You could see the rising of her chest as it moved quickly up and down.

Stanley broke the kiss and looked Tamara in the eyes.

"Are you okay?"

Tamara laughed as she fanned herself.

"I wasn't expecting that!"

Stanley pulled his shirt from inside his pants to hide his huge bulge.

CHAPTER 4

Thomas sat outside of Tamara's home as he tried to talk himself out of going inside and confessing his love to her. As he continued to sit, his phone rang. He looked at the phone and saw it was Sherry.

"Yes, Sherry."

"Are you inside yet?"

"No, I'm still inside the car."

"Boy, if you don't get your big ass out of that car and let that woman know how you feel!"

"Okay, okay, I'm going," Thomas said as he got out and walked up to the front door.

"I'll call you later," He disconnected the call.

Thomas knocked twice before Tamara answered.

"Hey Thomas, what are you doing here?"

"Are you busy?"

"I have company, but come on in."

As Thomas stepped foot inside, he looked up and saw Stanley standing there. His heart shattered.

"Thomas, this is Stanley, and Stanley this is my radio
co-host and good friend."

"Hey, have are you?" Stanley asked.

Thomas was so shocked, he could only nod his head.

He looked over at Tamara, "I see you're busy, so I'll talk to you another time."

"Are you sure?" She could sense something was troubling her good friend.

"Yeah, it's nothing. I will talk with you at work tomorrow," Thomas said as he looked over at Stanley and back at Tamara.

"Okay, have a good evening," Tamara said as she walked Thomas out and watched him as he drove off.

When Tamara walked back inside, she found Stanley just standing smiling.

"Why are you smiling?"

Stanley chuckled, "How long has he been in love with you?"

"Whoa! What are you talking about?"

"Come on, Tamara. It's written all over his face. He was disappointed when he saw me standing here."

"No, he's probably having problems with one of his female friends."

"Okay, if you say so, but a man knows when another man is in love with someone."

"You don't know Thomas, but I do. When I first met him, I had a crush on him, but he never gave me the time of day."

"Really?"

"Yes, really," Tamara said as she sat on the couch.

The next day, Tamara saw Thomas as soon as she stepped foot in the break room. She walked over to him.

"Hey, are you okay?" She asked as she grabbed hold of his arm."

Thomas moved his arm from her grip, "Why wouldn't I be?" He said as he walked out of the break room.

Tamara removed her coat, purse, and put them into her locker before heading over to pour herself a cup of coffee.

She felt bad that she wasn't there for Thomas when he came to her yesterday.

When Tamara walked into the studio, Thomas never looked up.

"Hey, did I do something wrong?"

Thomas looked up at Tamara. He saw the concerned look on her face. He stood up and walked over to her, bent down and wrapped his arms around her.

"I'm sorry for being so cold to you. You didn't deserve that. Please accept my apology."

"Sure," Tamara said.

"Is that your new dude I saw yesterday?"

"No, we are just friends. He was the girl's substitute teacher. They set us up."

"Oh yeah. Do you like him?"

"So far, he seems pretty cool."

Tamara looked at Thomas when she thought about what Stanley said about Thomas.

"You know, he told me he thought you were in love with me. Imagine that."

Thomas looked at Tamara as he slipped on his headphones. He never said one way or another if Stanley was wrong. Thomas allowed her to think what she wanted to think.

Thomas knew he was wrong for taking his frustrations out on Tamara, he had himself to blame for not pursuing her early on.

That evening, Tamara met Stanley for dessert at the Cheesecake factory.

"How was your day?" Stanley asked.

"It was good. How was yours?

"It was fantastic since I knew I would be seeing you," Stanley said.

"Same here," Tamara said. "So, what are you doing for Thanksgiving? Tamara asked, hoping he would say he was spending it alone.

"I don't know. I haven't even thought about it."

"Okay, it's settled. You can spend Thanksgiving with me, the girls, my family, and friends."

"Only if you let me help in the kitchen."

"Do you know your way around the kitchen?" Tamara asked.

"Don't let these good looks fool you. I am good at everything I do. I mean everything," Stanley said as he smiled flirtatiously at Tamara as he licked his lips.

"Okay, I am going to hold you to that."

The next day at work, Thomas was still acting weird with Tamara. On their fifteen-minute break, she followed Thomas down the hall into the break room.

"What are you doing this evening?" Tamara asked Thomas.

Thomas hesitated a little too long for Tamara.

"Thomas, what the fuck is wrong with you!" Tamara was frustrated and walked out of the break room.

This is the reason Thomas never pursued Tamara because if things didn't work out, it would make working conditions difficult for them both.

Later that evening, Tamara canceled her dinner date with Stanley. Instead, she visited her best friend Sherry's place.

Tamara arrived unannounced and hoped Sherry didn't have one of her young hot men over.

Tamara got out of the car and walked quickly to the front door. She knocked twice before Sherry answered.

"What's the surprise visit for?"

"I'm sorry, but I need to talk with you."

"Don't be sorry. You know you're always welcome over here. I am just surprised because you always call first."

"I know, I was in such a hurry that I didn't think to call."

"Have a seat while I fix us a drink."

Two minutes later, Sherry walked back into the room with two glasses of Mango Moscato.

She handed a glass to Tamara and took a seat right next to her.

"Now, what seems to be the problem?"

"Have you spoken with Thomas?"

"Yes, why?"

"He has been very cold and distant to me. You would think I did something to him. Has he said anything to you about me?"

Sherry hesitated to answer.

"Yes, he has said something to me, but trust me, it's not really you, it's him. You have done nothing."

"Well, what is the problem?"

"I think you need to have a heart-to-heart talk with Thomas and hopefully he will be honest and tell you what's going on."

CHAPTER 5

The next day, Tamara and Stanley had a cooking date. He was at his place and she was at her place in the kitchen. They face-timed each other as they prepared their dinner.

"So, Mr. cook so good. What's on your menu?"

"I already started cooking my fried Chicken. I'm making some fried Kale, and some buttery crispsy smashed potato's with some cornbread muffins."

"Oh, wow! You got my mouth watering over here."

"Just wait until you taste it."

Stanley moved his phone closer. He showed her his golden crispy fried chicken.

"Damn, my chicken smells good."

"It looks delicious," Tamara said.

"What's on your menu?"

"Nothing special just some Rib Eye steaks sauteed with some onions and mushrooms. Fried potatoes, fried biscuits, and a side salad."

"Dang."

"I know, right. And it smells so good."

"Those fried biscuits will go good with

my dish," Stanley said.

"I'll save you some."

Just then the girls walked into the kitchen.

"Mom, who are you talking to?" Drake asked as she moved further into the room, and then she saw Mr. Clarke on the phone.

"Hey Mr. Clarke," Drake said.

"Mr. Clarke, whatcha cooking?" Blake asked.

Stanley rattled off what he was cooking.

"Mr. Clarke, can you save me and Blake some chicken and some of those smashed potato's?"

"I got you girls."

"Thanks," The girls said in unison.

Later that night, once Tamara settled into bed, she picked up her phone and called Stanley.

"You all settled in now?" Stanley asked.

"Yes. You know this was the first time I have ever cooked and face-timed someone. This was a great idea."

"This was my second time. The first time was with my aunt. She was guiding me through the process of making some homemade rolls."

"How did they turn out?"

Stanley laughed, "Horrible."

Tamara laughed.

Over the next couple of weeks, Stanley and Tamara began to spend a lot of time with each other.

Thomas accepted another position at another radio station. Tamara missed him dearly, but she was getting used to her new co-host.

Tamara had reached out to Thomas a couple of times to see how things were going, but her calls went straight to voicemail.

And then out of nowhere, one day, while Tamara was driving home, she received a call from an unknown number. She let it go to voicemail and when she arrived home, Thomas was parked in her driveway.

"I can't believe it. The dead has risen," Tamara said as she got out of her car. Tamara peered inside the car to see if Thomas was in there, but when she didn't see him, she knew he was inside.

As she opened the front door and walked in, she heard talking coming from the kitchen. She found Thomas, Blake and Drake are in the kitchen cooking.

"What in the world is going on in here?"

"Mom, Drake, and I wanted to prepare dinner for you, and uncle Thomas came to help us."

"Hey, how are you? Thomas asked.

"I'm good and you, stranger?"

Thomas wiped his hands off with the dishtowel and grabbed hold of Tamara's hand.

"Can we talk?"

"Sure. Let's go into the living room."

Thomas and Tamara sat down right next to each other.

"I want to start by apologizing to you. I know I have been an ass to you and you did nothing to deserve it. You're one of my best friends who has always had my back."

"Yes, you were an ass and yes, I will always have your back. Thomas, you can come and talk to me about anything."

Thomas hesitated to speak.

"What is it, Thomas?"

Thomas leaned his head back against the couch and closed his eyes.

"From the very first time I laid eyes on you. I wanted you to be mine, but I fucked up. I didn't want a relationship with anyone that I worked with and now that I am no longer there, you're seeing someone. It's been eating me up inside to know I let you slip right through my fingers. I didn't know how to handle it. That's why I acted the way I did."

This news blew Tamara away.

"Wow!" She said as she began to blush.

"I never knew you felt that way. It's funny because I felt the same way you felt when I first saw you. I flirted with you a little to see if you would take the bait, but when you didn't, I moved on."

"Damn! See, you should have told me."

"Right, just like you should have told me."

"Well, it's too late for the shoulda, coulda, and woulda's, what are we going to do about it now?" Thomas asked.

"We can't do anything about it, since I am seeing someone now."

"I'm willing to fight for what I want. I am in love with you."

Tamara looked at Thomas. She could see the sincerity and sadness in his eyes.

"So, why now? Why would you wait to tell me this now! Now that I am seeing someone. I don't get it. How long have we worked together and you never said shit! Don't do this to me now, Thomas!"

Tamara stood. She paced back and forth.

In the meantime, the girls were ear hustling from the kitchen.

"Wow, uncle Thomas is in love with our mom," Blake said.

"Now I feel awful that we set her up with

Mr. Clarke," Drake said.

"Well, at least there are people interested in her now.

You know that old saying that once you find someone everyone comes out of the woodwork to try and talk to you," Blake said.

Drake looked at her sister sideways.

"I've never heard that. You need to stop sitting around old people and listening to their conversations," Drake said.

"Girl whatever!"

Thomas stood and pulled Tamara to him. He bent down and tried to kiss Tamara, but she took a step back.

"Thomas, I can't do this. I am interested in Stanley, I am sorry."

Thomas stood there with his broken heart in his hand.

Later that night, Tamara placed a call to Sherry.

"Girl, I can't believe you knew Thomas was into me. You are so wrong because you knew how I felt about him and you said nothing."

"It wasn't my place to tell you," Sherry said with an attitude.

"What's wrong with you?"

"We have a bad habit of falling for the same people and who always ends up with them, not me. So why would I tell you Thomas was in love with you. I told him to tell you how he felt and he didn't until now. So now you know."

"Um... so are we best friends or not? Tell me so I know how to play my hand."

"I'm sorry Tamara, you just caught me at a bad time."
Tamara was a little irritated at this point with Sherry.

"I'll let you go, but if you want Thomas, go for it." Tamara disconnected the call.

The next evening while having dinner at Stanley's Tamara figured she would fill him in on what was going on.

"I told you that man was in love with you and as long as he is in love with you, your friend won't stand a chance with him."

"I hope you're wrong. Because she seems to be really into him."

"Well, we will just see how everything plays out, but in the meantime, I need to know how you feel now that you know how he feels about you? Do I have a reason to worry?"

"No, you don't have anything to worry

47

about," Tamara said as she got up to moved and stand in front of Stanley and wrapped her arms around him.

"I told him that I chose you."

"Now, that's what I wanted to hear," Stanley said as he brushed his lips up against hers.

Tamara opened her mouth to let Stanley enter. Stanley deepened the kiss as his hands moved down to her rear end. A moan escaped Tamara's mouth.

CHAPTER 6

Two weeks later, Sherry and Thomas arrived at Tamara. She was shocked since she hadn't spoken to Sherry since that phone conversation she had with her about Thomas.

"I am so surprised to see you two," Tamara said as she stood at the front door.

"Come on in and get out of the cold. And before I forget, you guys are invited to my Thanksgiving dinner. Dinner will start at five this year."

"Why thank you," Sherry said as she hugged Tamara. I'm sorry about our last phone conversation," She whispered into Tamara's ear.

Tamara waved her hand in the air, "Girl, don't worry about that."

Sherry and Thomas sat on the couch. Tamara noticed how close they were sitting to each other.

"Well, we wanted to tell you this before you heard it from someone else. We are together," Thomas said.

"What do you mean together?"

"Together as in a couple," Sherry said.

Tamara was taken back, "Oh, okay.

When did this happen?"

"Two weeks ago?" Sherry said.

"Two weeks ago," Tamara said. Then she remembered that was right after she told Thomas she was seeing Stanley. Oh, she's the rebound, she thought to herself.

"Well, I am happy for you both."
Just then, she heard the doorbell.

"That must be Stanley," Tamara said as she got up to answer the door.
Sherry noticed how Thomas looked at Tamara but then blew it off.

"Thomas, you remember Stanley, right?"

"Yes, hey, how are you doing?"

"I'm good."

"And this is my friend Sherry."
Sherry noticed how Tamara introduced her as a friend when she would normally introduce her as her best friend.
Stanley removed his coat and hung it on the coat rack.

"Would you two care for some wine," He said as he looked at Thomas and Sherry.

"I would," Thomas said.
Sherry eyed Thomas and then whispered to him.

"I thought we were going back to my place?"

Thomas was too busy eyeing Tamara that he didn't hear what Sherry had asked him. Sherry became angry, but she didn't want to show it.

"I'll have some too," Sherry said.
Sherry got up and walked over to Tamara.

"Hey, can I have a word with you in private?"

"Sure."
Sherry and Tamara went upstairs to Tamara's bedroom.
Once inside, Sherry moved and stood in front of Tamara.

"Hey, are you okay with Thomas and I?"

"Why wouldn't I be?"

"I just want to make sure we are okay, since you introduced me as your friend and not your best friend as you always do."

"Well, after our phone conversation two weeks ago, and since I hadn't heard from you, I wasn't sure we were still best friends. To be honest, I feel as though you're competing with me and that's not how I want our friendship to be."

"What! Why do you say that?"

"Come on girl, you know every man that likes me, you like, and it's always some confusion with us about someone I'm not even interested in.

You start trying to be someone you're not. You know how I talk about writing my novel, and now you want to write a novel. If I take a dance class the next week, you take one. I work as a radio host and all of a sudden, you want to start a BlogTalkRadio show and host it. This goes on and on, and normally I wouldn't pay it any attention, but this time it bothers me."

"Well, I am sorry you feel that way, but forgive me for wanting to have some hobbies or reach goals."

"Girl, you never speak of any of these things until I do, so how can they be your goals?"

Just then, there's a knock at the door.

Tamara opened the door to find Thomas standing.

"Is everything okay?"

"Yes, why wouldn't it be. We will be down in a few."

Tamara shut the door back.

"You know, I'm a little irritated because Thomas was angry with me, and then you had an attitude with me the last time we talked, and for what? I have done nothing to either of you. You guys took shit out on me because of your issues that have nothing to do with me and I don't appreciate it!"

Sherry moved closer to Tamara, "You're right and I am sorry. A best friend doesn't act like this. Will you forgive me?" Sherry wiped the tears from Tamara's eyes.

"I don't know, should I," Tamara said as she cracked a smile.

"Yes, you should," Sherry said as she started to tickle Tamara.

"Okay, okay, I forgive you guys," Tamara said as she tried to get away from Sherry.

Later that night, Stanley helped Tamara with her overnight bag. This would be the first time that they spent the night with each other. This would also be the first time at his home. As Tamara walked in she checked out the décor, she was very impressed. It has a homey feel to it, but still had a masculine touch to it.

"Ooh, I really like this. Let me guess, you did the decorating?"

"Of course."

"You did a great job. How many bedrooms?"

"Five."

Tamara did a double-take, "Why so many rooms.

"I'm a family man, so whenever my family comes, I want to have plenty of room for them to spend the night if needed."

"Well, that makes sense. Can I get a tour?"

"You can get anything you want, and I mean anything."

They both laughed.

Later that night in bed, Tamara was a little nervous.

"God! It's been so long since I've been intimate with someone."

"Don't worry, I'll be gentle. I'll put your body and mind at ease," Stanley whispered as he kissed his way down her body. When he came to that spot, he opened her lips and let his tongue do what it do, and a moan escaped from Tamara's mouth.

"Oh my God! Stanley, please, I need you inside me!"

Stanley stuck the head of his nine and a half inches in, Tamara tried to get away.

"Don't run, baby, it's just the head."

Stanley eased inside of her hot box and begin to move slowly in and out.

"Shit, you feel so damn good!"

Stanley rolled over and pull Tamara with him until she was on top. Tamara took

control and rode him. She began to twerk
that ass on him. She moved up and down
and squeezed her pussy walls around him
each time she rose up. Stanley placed each
hand on each side of her body and moved
her up and down faster and faster until they
both came with pleasure.

CHAPTER 7

Tamara walked down the stairs to find Stanley in the kitchen preparing breakfast.

"Man, it smells so good in here," Tamara said as she walked up behind Stanley and wrapped her arms around his waist.

"I hope you enjoy it."

"From the way it smells, I can't help but enjoy it."

"Have a seat and I will bring a plate to you."

Stanley sat and watched as Tamara took a bite of his homemade Hashbrown casserole.

"Wow! This is so good. I'm going to need more of this."

Stanley laughed.

"You can have as much as you want."

Thomas and Sherry lay in bed both looking up at the ceiling without saying a word. They both had things on their mind.

Sherry decided to break the silence. She turned on her side to face Thomas, who was still looking up.

"What's on your mind?"

"What makes you think something is on my mind?"

"Because you're quiet, and besides, I know when something is bothering you."
Thomas looked over at Sherry and then back up at the ceiling.

"Well, since you won't tell me what's wrong. I am going to tell you what's wrong with me."
Thomas raised up and fluffed his pillows. He laid his back up against them. "What's wrong with you this time?"

"What do you mean this time

"There is always something wrong with you. You're never satisfied."
Thomas chuckled.

"Oh, so that's how you see things?"

"Pretty much."
Sherry was lit. She hopped out of bed and reached for her clothing.

"So you're not going to tell me what's wrong."

"Oh, no! I wouldn't want to be complaining or seem not satisfied."

"Woman, if you don't tell me what's wrong."

"Why did you ask me to be with you? Was it because Tamara is with someone?"

"What are you talking about?"

"I saw the way you kept staring at her

57

last night. I don't want to be anyone's second choice."

"Second choice. You already knew who I wanted to be with, and have for some time now. So anyone that I am with will be my second choice. I don't know what to say. As I said, you knew who had my heart."

"You don't have to make me feel like a second choice."

"I didn't know I was making you feel like that. I apologize if you feel that way. If I didn't care about you, you wouldn't even be here, right now."

"You care about me all you want, but I want you to care about me as your lady and not your friend."

"I don't fuck my friends!"

"So, that's what we did fucked? What about making love?"

"Are we in love? So until we are in love, we fuckin!"

"Wow!"

"So you don't agree?"

"No, I don't agree. I have been in love with you far as long as you have been in love with Tamara."

"Well, if you still think I am in love with Tamara, why would you want to be with me? Is this a competition or something?"

"Ugh, there you go! Look, I ain't playing second to no one."

"Well, I don't know what to tell you. I mean I care for you and all, but you already know the deal."

Sherry continued to get dressed.

"I'm out of here!" Sherry walked out and slammed the door behind her.

"Women. You can't live with them, and you can't live without them," Thomas said as he got out of bed and went into the restroom.

"Stanley, what do you want to do today?"

"Let's go bowling. I haven't done that in a long time."

"That sounds like a good idea. Why don't we invite Thomas and Sherry? It will be us against them, or the men against the women."

"Here I sent you Thomas's number so you can call and ask him."

Stanley phoned Thomas but he didn't get an answer.

"He didn't answer so I will send him a text."

Five minutes later, Thomas replied back.

"What time?"

"Oh, he just responded back.

He wants to know what time?"

"Um… let's say around 7."

Later that evening, It started out with the men against the women, and the men killed the women. Then they decided to have couples against couples, and Thomas and Sherry won three games.

"Man, I am worn out," Tamara said.

"I think your ball was way too heavy."

"Yeah, it was heavy."

Stanley pulled into Tarmar's driveway. He cut the ignition. He reached over and turned Tamara's face to face him with his finger.

"You know I have had the best time of my life since meeting you, and I hope you feel the same way."

"I do. I never thought I could care for someone as much as I care for you."

"Well, with that being said, I think we should take this to the next level. I want to be in an exclusive relationship with you."

"I will have to second that," Tamara said as she leaned in to meet Stanley's lips.

Thomas and Sherry decided to grab some food from J's Seafood and Wings.

"Man, this food smells so damn good?" Sherry said.

"I can't believe you have never had the wings before," Thomas said as he shook his head.

"Well, if they are as good as you say, I will be their number one customer because I love me some wings," Sherry said.

Thomas laughed.

"Did you have a good time this evening?"

"Yes, I did. And I also noticed how you went out of your way to make me feel like your number one. I appreciate that," Sherry said as she gave Thomas that pretty smile.

"If I am with you, it's because I want to be with you. I could have chosen someone else, but I chose you, whether you were my first choice or not."

"How would you feel if I told you were my second choice?"

"It wouldn't bother me because I know I could be your final choice."

"Oh really, are you that sure of yourself?"

"You damn right I am. I know what I can do in the bedroom, and outside the bedroom," Thomas said as he winked at her.

61

Tamara sat in bed as she talked with Stanley.

"How flexible is your work schedule around New Year's eve?"

"It's pretty flexible, why?"

"Well, every year on New Year's eve, I fly out to New York and bring in the new year there, and I would love for you to come with me this year."

"Oh my God, that sounds awesome."

"I'll pay for everything. You won't have to do anything but just be ready when I pick you up. I'll book the hotel and the air tomorrow if that's okay with you?"

"Are you serious?"

"Yeah."

"I've never had anyone to do something special like this for me"

"You deserve to be treated like the queen that you are."

"Why thank you, Mr. Stanley Clarke."

CHAPTER 8

Thomas and Sherry sat at the table eating.

"I'm glad you talked me into getting three different kinds of flavors. I don't know which one I like the best."

"The Garlic Saranchi is my favorite and then their honey barbeque."

"Yeah, that garlic Saranchi is fire!"

"So what do you think about Stanley Clarke?" Sherry asked to see if there was any jealousy in his tone."

"I think he's cool. I'm glad Tamara found someone that will treat her nice because she deserves it."

"What at about you? Do you think he's a good guy?"

"Umph, He seems okay."
Thomas looked at Sherry. Her tone seemed to be filled with a little envy and her next words confirmed his suspicion.

"She always gets the good guys while I get the ones that can't have her."
Thomas looked at her, "I beg your pardon."

"Oh, I'm sorry. I was just thinking out loud."

"Are you referring to me?"

"No, I was just thinking about the last three guys I dated. They all wanted her, but she wouldn't give them the time of day so they came to me."

Thomas was irritated. "Have you figured out why they approached her first and not you?"

Sherry looked at Thomas, "What are you trying to say?"

"I said what I was trying to say." Thomas stopped himself, but decided she needed to hear this, "Maybe if you would stop trying to compete with her and be happy, just maybe things would work out for you," Thomas said as he tossed his napkin on his plate and got up from the table.

"I think it's best that I leave before I say something that I might regret."

A couple of weeks had gone by and Sherry had not heard anything from Thomas. She hadn't reached out to Tamara either and every time Tamara tried to call, Sherry would let it go to voicemail.

It was the evening before Thanksgiving and Tamara and Stanley were in the kitchen cooking. Stanley helped her prep onions, celery, green peppers, and peel some potatoes.

"Man, I can taste these sweet potato pies now."

Tamara laughed. "Does your mom usually make them?"

"She used to, but now she makes Chess and pumpkin pies."

Two hours later, Tamara walked Stanley to the front door. They kissed good night and she stood in the door and watched as he pulled away. She wanted him to spend the night, but since her girls were home, they decided against it.

The next morning, Tamara was up early getting everything together. She wanted everything to be ready before her guest arrived. She also wanted to be dressed because like always, Thomas always arrive early, but seeing that he was seeing Sherry, she figured he would be late because Sherry was always late.

An hour before her guest were to arrive, Tamara called Sherry, and again it went straight to voicemail.

"Something is not right," Tamara said as she walked downstairs to the kitchen. She took her Mac and cheese out of the oven and set it on the stove, and when she turned around, there stood Thomas.

Tamara jumped, "Boy, what are you doing just standing there?"

Thomas laughed as he moved further into the kitchen and hugged Tamara. Tamara looked around Thomas expecting to see Sherry.

"Where's Sherry?"

"She's not in my back pocket," Thomas said as he looked behind him.

"What happened?"

"I'm tired of her trying to compete with you. She can't let it go that I wanted you over her. She keeps bringing up the fact that she was my second choice. I don't have time for that. I tried to show her that she had my attention and that she could have my heart, but she can't let it go."

"Okay, that explains everything."

"What do you mean."

"I have called and called her and it goes straight to voicemail. She will not return any of my calls."

"I believe she is secretly jealous of you, what kind of friend is that?"

Tamara shook her head. "I hate that it has to be that way, because she is a really good person if she could let go of that jealousy. That's why her sister doesn't deal with her.

She is jealous of her. Well, since you're here early as usual can you help set the table?"

"Sure."

"So how are things going with you and Stanley," Thomas asked.

Tamara smiled from ear to ear, "It is going very well. I never thought I could feel this way again."

"That's good, but if he messes up, it's over for him, I promise you that."

Stanley walked in on their conversation, "But I won't mess up."

Tamara and Thomas both turned at the sound of Stanley's voice.

"I was just saying, man."

"It's all good," Stanley said as he moved to hug and kiss Tamara on the lips. Stanley knew this would piss Thomas off.

Thomas never looked up. He continued to set the table.

An hour later, all of the guests had arrived and were sitting at the table eating and talking.

"Where's Sherry?" Tamara's cousin asked her.

"I don't know," Tamara said. She didn't want to get into a conversation about Sherry.

67

"She may come later, then again, she may not."

"Tamara, as always, the food is delicious. Now I'm ready for dessert," Tamara's mother said.

Tamara got up from the table. She knew her parents wanted to grill Stanley a little bit so she gave them some time with him.

"So, what are your intentions with my daughter?" Tamara's dad asked.

Stanley laughed. "I have only good intentions for her and her girls. I am very fond of all three of them."

"Where did you guys meet?" Her mom asked him.

"Actually, your granddaughter's set us up. I was their substitute teacher for a few months."

The girls laughed.

"They told their mom one thing and told me another."

"Well, I guess you're okay if the girls like you."

"Yeah, he's cool," Blake said.

Tamara walked back in with a piece of pie for her mother. I have cut you guys a piece of potato pie and a piece of cheesecake."

"Stanley, will you help me give everyone their dessert."

Later that evening, the girl's father stopped by and picked them up. They were spending the week with him. They were so excited to go shopping on Black Friday. Tamara's parents and cousins left an hour ago, so that left Tamara, Stanley, and Thomas.

"So, are you guys going shopping early tomorrow morning like everybody else?" Thomas asked.

"Yes, we are going shopping, then we're having breakfast and then were are coming back home and putting up the tree. You know I might even get a new tree if I can catch one on sale," Tamara said.

"What about you?" Stanley asked Thomas.

"Nah, I'm ordering my stuff on Cyber Monday."

CHAPTER 9

Black Friday rolled around, and Tamara and Stanley had been out shopping for hours. When they finally made it home, they were both too tired to put up the tree that Tamara bought on sale.

Before arriving home, they stopped at Crackle Barrel and ordered some Fried Chicken to go with the leftovers Thanksgiving meal. They sat in the recliners and ate as they watched a Christmas movie on the Hallmark channel and before they knew it, they both were asleep.

The ringing of Tamara's phone awoke her.

"Hey Thomas, what's up?"

"Have you heard from Sherry yet?"

"No, I haven't, why?"

"Her mom and sister just stopped by my place. They're worried. She didn't show up for dinner yesterday. Her car is in the driveway, but she's not answering her door or her phone."

"I have a spare key to her front door. I can let you in to see what's up. Give me about twenty minutes and I will meet you over there."

Tamara disconnected the call and nudged Stanley awake.

"Do you want to take a ride with me over to Sherry's? Something is not right, so I am going to meet Thomas over there and unlock her front door. Thomas said she never made it to her parent's house for dinner yesterday."

Thirty minutes later, Stanley and Tamara pulled into Sherry's driveway. Thomas got out of his car and met them at the front door. Tamara was nervous as she tried to unlock the door. Her hand began to shake, so Thomas took the key from her and inserted it into the lock. As soon as they opened the front door, the smell hit them right in their faces.
Tamara couldn't move. She was all too familiar with that smell. A year ago, Tamara found her baby brother dead in his apartment. He had been dead for a week and it turned out that his best friend murdered him over some drugs.

"Oh my God, no!" She screamed as she started to fall to the ground. Stanley caught her before she hit the ground.

"What is it?" Stanley asked.

"She's dead!" Tamara screamed.

Thomas looked at Tamara with fear on his face. Thomas ran upstairs to Sherry's bedroom and found her in bed. Both of her wrists had been slit.

"No! "No, Sherry!" Thomas screamed as he grabbed her up in his arms.
Stanley held onto Tamara as the tears ran down her face.
Minutes later, Sherry's family walked through the door, and by the way, Thomas looked and the way Tamara was crying, they knew it was not good.
Sherry's mother grabbed her chest, "Oh God, no! No!
Thomas held onto her. "I'm sorry Mrs. Smith."

A week later, they laid Sherry to rest. Tamara prepared food for the repass, and invited everyone to her home. She was trying to be strong, but she already felt the loss of her best friend.
Stanley walked into the kitchen and saw Tamara at the kitchen sink just standing there looking into space.

"Hey babe, are you doing okay?"
Tamara turned at the sound of Stanley's voice.

"No, why didn't I do something about

72

Sherry's issues?"

"What could you have done. You can only make a person get help if that's what they want."

"But I could have told her family."

"I'm pretty sure they already knew she had issues.
These issues didn't just start. They probably came from her childhood and got worse as she got older."
Stanley grabbed a napkin and wiped Tamara's tears away.
Thomas stood in the kitchen's entry and watched the interaction between Stanley and Tamara.
Tamara just happened to look up to see Thomas and to see the sadness in his eyes.
Tamara walked over to him and hugged him.

"I know you feel just as bad as I do, but we will get through this together," Tamara whispered.
Stanley watched. He didn't know if he should be upset or understanding, but he decided on the latter.

The next couple of weeks, Tamara and Thomas checked upon each other. It seemed that Sherry's death brought them closer to each other like they used to be.

73

On Friday, Stanley had to go out of town to visit his family so Thomas helped Tamara wrap her Christmas gifts.

"So, what did you get me?"

"Like I'm going to tell you. You will have to wait until Christmas like everyone else. I swear, sometimes you act just like my teenagers.

"Damn! That was a hard blow."

"Whatever," Tamara said as she playfully pushed Thomas.

It was Christmas eve, and Stanley and Tamara were in the kitchen preparing for their first Christmas dinner together.

"Man, this eggnog is so good. I could drink this entire bottle," Tamara said.

"Go right ahead. I'll continue to sip on this peach Moscato wine. Now, this is the bomb, especially since it's a little slushy," Stanley said.

"Hey, can you cut up some celery and green peppers for me and that should do it for tonight?" Tamara asked.

Once the couple was finished in the kitchen, they sat on the couch by the fireplace drinking and listening to some Christmas music.

"Don't forget at midnight, we get to open one of our gifts," Tamara said.

"Oh shit, I almost forgot. I need to run home right quick and I will be right back," Stanley said as he got up from the couch.

Tamara followed Stanley to the front door and kissed him, "Now you hurry on back, okay."

They both decided that it was time to let the girls get used to having Stanley spend the night.

Tamara stood in the door until Stanley was out of sight.

She rushed upstairs and ran her a nice hot bath. She wanted to be fresh and clean for the man of her dreams.

When Tamara got out of the tub, she noticed the time.

She picked up her phone to see if she had missed a call from him, but there were no missed call. She walked into the girl's room and looked out the window to see if his car was outside, and it wasn't.

Tamara went back to her room and called Stanley, but she got no answer so she left him a message.

Thirty minutes later, still no word from Stanley. Tamara began to worry. She called him again, and again, and still no answer.

Tamara walked to the door and stood looking out when it started to snow.

Two hours had gone by and still no word from Stanley so she decided to go to bed. She figured she would just see him in the morning.

Tamara laid down and went to sleep. She awoke at 4 am.

She looked at her phone and still no missed calls. She called Stanley again and still no answer.

At 6 am Tamara got up and fixed some coffee and that's when she broke down.

"God, what is going on?" She cried softly to herself.

Tamara sat for an hour at the kitchen table sipping on her coffee wondering what was going on when she remembered one of her gifts from Stanley.

Tamara walked over to the tree and grabbed one of the gifts Stanley had placed under the tree for her and opened it. She cried as she laid eyes on a diamond ring. It was the most beautiful ring she had ever laid eyes on. She couldn't tell if it was an engagement ring or not, but at this point, it didn't matter.

At noon, Tamara phoned Stanley again. She called him again at 3 before her family was expected to arrive and still no answer.

"Stanley, where are you?"

Just then, her girls walked down. "Mom, where is Mr. Clarke?" Blake asked.

"I don't know."

The girls looked at each other.

"Mom, are you okay?" Drake asked.

"Yes, baby, I'm just tired."

"Do you need us to do anything?"

"No, but thanks. Everything is done."

They heard a knock at the front door and Tamara's heart did flip flops. She smiled the biggest smile for it to turn into a frown. It was her sister and two cousins.

"Dang, don't look so happy to see us."

"I'm sorry, I was just expecting it to be Stanley."

"Don't tell me you guys have had your first argument."

"No, nothing like that. Actually, everything has been too good to be true with us."

Later that evening after everyone had gone home. Thomas stayed back to talk to Tamara. He pulled her to the couch, "So what's going on?"

"I hate to say this, but I think Stanley ghosted me."

"What! No way."

"Yes. He left last night to go home and to get something. He was supposed to come right back and I have not heard from him. I continue to call his phone and he doesn't answer. " At this point, she breaks down. Thomas pulled her close to him.

"Do you want to go to his place to see what is going on?"

"No, not right now. What if he doesn't want to see me? He is the one that has disappeared not me. I want him to come to me and explain to me what is going on."

"I understand."

CHAPTER 10

It was New Year's eve and still no word from Stanley. Tamara was very disappointed and sad because she and Stanley would have been in New York by now getting ready to bring in the new year, but instead, she's home alone with no one to bring in the new year with. Her girls were at a sleepover down the street, Sherry was gone and she had no idea what Thomas is up to.

It was ten minutes before the new year. Tamara sat on the couch staring at the TV when she heard a knock at her front door. Her heart began to beat rapidly, her thoughts of Stanley at the door flooded her mind. She opened the door quickly to find Thomas with a party hat on and a couple of bottles of wine.

"Now, did you think I was going to let you bring in the new year by yourself?" Tamara smiled a weak smile.

"I'm glad you thought about me," Tamara said as she allowed Thomas to enter. Tamara grabbed the bottles of wine and walked into the kitchen. Thomas followed behind her and placed a party hat on top of her head.

"Let's get this party started," Thomas said loudly as he did a dance move.

"You know you look crazy, right." Tamara laughed.

"Don't hate!

Tamara poured a glass of wine for herself and Thomas and walked into the living room just in time for the countdown.

Thomas grabbed Tamara's drink from her hand and set it down on the end table. He pulled her up close to him as they counted down to the new year. The sounds of gunshots filled the air as Thomas held onto Tamara and looked down into her eyes.

"Happy New Year, Tamara."

Tamara looked up at Thomas, "Happy New Year to you too, Thomas," Tamara said.

Thomas bent down and kissed Tamara on the lips.

His lips were soft Tamara thought.

"You know I told you if Stanley ever messed up, I was moving in and I meant that."

Tamara laid her head against Thomas's chest as the tears rolled down her face.

They stood there moving back and forth to the smooth sound of Darnell Jones's 'Where

I Want to Be.' Thomas was in heaven while Tamara felt like she was in hell. She missed Stanley so much. She never thought she could love like this again, but Stanley came in and showed her how to love again.

Many thoughts went through her head as to why he disappeared. It just didn't make any sense to her.

Over the next couple of weeks, Tamara and Thomas had been hanging out. She still missed Stanley, but each day got better. One day, in particular, Thomas had come over and he sat her down.

"There's something I want to talk with you about?"

"Is everything okay?"

"Yes, things couldn't be better."

Thomas had this serious look on his face as he gazed at her.

"Okay, spill it," Tamara said.

Thomas hesitated, "Uh, you know, uh."

"Boy, if you don't tell me what's going on!" Tamara yelled.

"Tamara, I want to take you out on a date. A real date."

Tamara looked at Thomas. She saw a shy side of him that she had never seen before.

"I can't believe you did all of that just to ask me out on a date. I thought you had something serious to ask me."

"That's serious to me."

"Sure, I will go out with you."

"I mean a real date, Tamara. Not us going out as friends. I want it to be more than just friends if that's possible."

Tamara looked at Thomas and smiled which melted his heart.

"But first, I want you to get closure with Stanley. I don't want any chances that you guys will get back together."

"That's not going to happen. I never thought he would do me like this and if he did it once, he will do it again. But I agree, I do need closure."

The next week, Thomas rode with Tamara over to Stanley's. She pulled into the driveway behind another car, but she didn't see his car.

"Don't be nervous, just do what you came to do," Thomas said.

"Okay, well here it goes," Tamara said as she got out of the car and made her way to the front door.

Before Tamara could knock, the door opened and there stood a very attractive woman.

"Hi, can I help you?" The lady asked.

"Yes, I'm here to see Stanley," Tamara said nervously.

The woman studied Tamara, "Are you, Tammy?"

"No, I'm Tamara."

"Oh, I'm sorry, but that's what I meant."

"I'm Stanley's sister."

Tamara smiled.

"We didn't know how to get in contact with you."

"Contact me for what?"

The sister saw the fear on Tamara's face. And Tamara saw tears form in the sister's eyes.

"Is everything okay?" Tamara asked. "Where is Stanley?"

The sister put her hands up to her mouth as her husband stepped into view.

"On Christmas eve, Stanley was on his way home when he had a fatal accident," The brother-in-law said.

Tamara felt as though the wind had been knocked out of her. She couldn't breathe, things started to spin around her, and all of a sudden, she screamed, "NO! NO!" Tamara's legs gave way and she fell to the ground.

Thomas hopped out of the car in record time and helped the brother-in-law picked Tamara up.

She cried like a baby in Thomas's arms.

While Stanley's sister cried in her husbands' arms.

Over the next couple of weeks, Tamara and Thomas's relationship had deepened, but she still missed Stanley. She was thankful for him coming into her life and helping her see that she could love again. She will always keep a special place in her heart for him.

Sometimes when a person enters your life, it doesn't mean they are there to stay. Some people are only there for a season or a reason.

THE CHRISTMAS BREAK-UP

CHAPTER 1

Allyssa Peterson used strong strides as she walked through her five-thousand square foot home giving meticulous inspection in every room. Everything needed to look perfect. She took great pride in the home that she decorated which spawned her interior decorating business in six short years. She started out as a homemaker, but as her two children Riann and Allen grew older and eventually left for college, she was bored and needed a hobby to keep her mind off being lonely. After all, her husband Randall was never home anyway. He was always "busy" being an account executive for a major law firm.

Allyssa paused at the fireplace mantle in the family room to straighten a picture of their loving family during their earlier years. She smiled half-heartedly as she remembered that day in the park when she and Randall had decided to surprise the kids with an impromptu picnic in which Randall pretended to discover a box of water guns that were conveniently left in the park. Riann and Allen were only nine and seven at the time and were still very impressionable. Furthermore, Allyssa and Randall were at their best as far as their relationship was concerned. That was when Randall was working a regular accounting job, and still trying to figure out exactly what he wanted to do with his career. They didn't have much, but they had each other, and Allyssa was perfectly happy to be Mrs. Randall Peterson.

Although a few people, including certain members of her family, had an issue with them being an interracial couple, Allyssa felt as though she was on top of the world. Randall being an up-and-coming African American man working in a predominantly white law firm as an accountant seemed impossible at first. She used to worry at times that someone would flex their white privilege and have him fired, but he soon proved his value, and she was impressed with his ambition as well as his success as he was promoted to his current position as their lead accountant that oversaw all the finances for the company.

They had met in the nineties on their

college campus. Randall was standing on a platform talking about the injustices that black men endure while using Rodney King's brutal beat down as a prime example since the officers had been found not guilty in the recent months prior and the city of LA was in a total uproar, where an additional sixty-three people had been killed during the riots. It was something in the way his velvety smooth voice sounded as he spoke passionately about the events that grabbed her attention. He was the true definition of tall, dark, and handsome. His thick, black, wavy hair was cut low to his head, and his blue V-neck t-shirt accented his skin tone to perfection. Not to mention, his broad shoulders and muscular physique were quite the turn-on. However, Allyssa was most impressed by his eloquent way of speaking. He wasn't arrogant or cocky, but rather his meek yet demanding posture that oozed with swagger made him the sexiest man she had ever seen.

Allyssa was quite a knock-out herself back then. While she only stood a mere 5'3 to his 6'3 height, her equally thick, long, brownish-black wavy hair draped to the middle of her back. Her perfectly tanned complexion gave her the appearance of golden glitter in Randall's eyes. She was gorgeous, and her spiritual energy was a magnetic force to be recognized instantly. They met for lunch after his speech and immediately hit it off. They would go on to complete college together. They married a couple of years later and proceeded to have two beautiful children, their daughter Riann and their son Allen.

They were always a close-knit family. Allyssa made sure of that. Especially since the majority of her family was less than enthused of her marrying a "Darkie" as they would call him when they thought she wasn't listening. Allyssa was beyond proud of her family and her accomplishments. So she thought it best to cut them off completely. She didn't want or need the approval of anyone so narrow-minded as to use race as a reason to dislike anyone. She loved Randall deeply. He took excellent care of their family, and that's all that mattered to her... until recently.

She was having trouble understanding the disconnect between them. Randall was never home anymore. Despite her pleadings with him to take vacations or be spontaneous in general, seemed to fall on deaf ears. She was growing tired of trying to pull any type of emotion out of him and felt that she lived in this beautiful mini-mansion alone. At first, they would just bicker at one another, then that turned into arguments, which turned into days without speaking to each other. Finally, after the kids went back to school, after Thanksgiving break, Allyssa asked him to move out and requested that they become separated. She didn't want to upset Riann and Allen, so they agreed to keep it between them for now, but she knew the time was coming to reveal it to them. With Randall being gone for almost a month, Allyssa felt justified in being alone and was ready to take the next step to divorce. It's not that she didn't love him anymore. She knew she still loved him, but she felt vindicated in her decision to be done with it since she felt he didn't care anyway.

Deep down, she knew that he loved her too. She just wasn't secure in believing that he was still "in love" with her. It's not that she felt that he had been unfaithful to her, at least she prayed he hadn't, but if he had, she would at least understand why he just stopped paying attention to her. As far as she knew, she had been the ideal wife. She was encouraging, supportive, she kept herself up, and tried to keep things spicy in the bedroom. Although, it was tough for her now that she was forty-seven, and her body had been going through a few changes, to say the least. Overall, she was in good health, and she did her best to keep up and be what the bible called a "help-mate" for her husband. She was a firm believer in the word of God and attended church regularly. But despite all her prayers, and trying everything that she knew how to do, she kept falling short of her engaging with her husband, and she was fed up with it.

"Where is he anyway?" She said aloud.

"He was supposed to be here an hour ago!" Frustrated, she stormed over to the dining room table, where she had laid her cellular phone down and snatched it up. She retrieved his number from her favorite contact list and drummed her perfectly polished fingernails across her tightly folded arms. Just as the number dialed, she heard the ring tone coming through the back door. Randall, being the type of individual that was laid back with a dry sense of humor, answered the phone anyway even though he was already in the house.

"Thank you for calling Pizza Kings. This is Randy, what can I place on order for you today?" He joked, hoping to lighten his wife's mood that he knew would be furious.

"OMG Randall! What took you so long? You were supposed to be here a long time ago. The kids are going to be here at any minute!" She didn't waste time laying into him. Randall, still hoping to make her smile, came through the kitchen doorway, with open arms holding a bouquet of yellow and red roses.

"Honey, I'm home." He knew he was taking a long shot by stating the obvious, but his sarcasm was somewhat on purpose, as he hadn't been home in nearly a month since she put him out. His heartstrings tugged at that thought, as he genuinely missed being there. He missed his wife, but he was merely trying to do whatever it took to make her happy by respecting her wishes. He desperately hoped that their time apart had made her heart grow fonder, and he smiled weakly hoping that she would show signs of softening. When her disgusted facial expression didn't change, his heart sank a little.

"Sorry, babe. I was…"

"Working! Yes! I already know." She finished his sentence and snatched the flowers out of his hand. "Did you at least remember to pick up the ham?"

"Ugh, sorry honey. I'll run and do that real quick." He started for his keys that he laid on the counter, but Allyssa held up her hands to stop him.

"You know what, don't bother! I knew I couldn't count on you to remember to do something simple, so I already handled it! I had one delivered earlier."

"So, why didn't you tell me?" Randall asked frustrated and defeated.

"Because it wouldn't have mattered. You clearly hear whatever you want, whenever it's convenient for you. Besides, I was curious to see if this time apart has made you any more aware of what I want, and what I need. And you proved my point perfectly, which is why I want to proceed with the divorce!"

Randall's heart sank to his feet. He stood in shock for a moment before he exploded with hurt and anger.

"Over a damn ham! Allyssa come on! Be reasonable! Of all the things I've done for you, that I DO for you, you want a divorce because I forgot a stupid ham?" His voice cracked a little.

"It's not about the damn ham Randall!"

Allyssa fired back. "It's the fact that you don't consider me at all! You put your work over everything, and you don't stop to think about the rest of us! I could see if you were cheating on me. I'd almost prefer another woman. At least then I would know what I was competing against. I'd know how to fight back. But with this, I feel like I'm swinging at myself in the dark. I can't fight what I can't see, and frankly, I'm tired of fighting!" She paused to lower her voice and catch her breath. "I'm tired, Randall. I think it's best that we go our separate ways so that we don't keep each other from being happy."

"Why do you think I do all of this? It's so that you and the kids can be HAPPY! So that if I die, you all will continue to live comfortably, and not have to worry about anything. Never once do you consider the sacrifices that I make, so that you can have all of this! This place is a palace compared to where I grew up! Do you think that I work for the 'fun' of it? I bust my ass day in and out so that you can live like a queen and not lift a finger, and so that the kids can have the luxuries that I could only dream about when I was their age. If anyone should feel unappreciated around here it should be me!" With that, he headed towards the back door again.

"Where are you going?" Allyssa called after him.

"To sit in MY backyard, that I PAY for, and haven't seen in a month because MY WIFE put me out of MY HOUSE!!"

"Listen here buddy, YOU'RE not the only one that pays for this house. You may handle the mortgage, but I MADE this HOUSE the HOME that IT IS! Only you wouldn't know that because even when you're here... YOU'RE NOT HERE!!!" She slammed the door behind him and ran to the powder room that was in the hallway off the kitchen.

All she could think to do was to splash cold water on her face. She took long deep breaths in through her nose, and out through her mouth to try to calm down. She wrung her hands together to stop them from shaking. She wanted to cry, but she refused the temptation as she knew that Allen and Riann would only be even more upset. Tonight was going to be difficult enough as it was trying to get through dinner without wanting to throttle Randall. She didn't even know how she was going to make it through the weekend. The plan was to get through

Christmas Day, and then tell them about the break-up, but with the way she was feeling at this moment, she had half the mind to tell them as soon as they walked in the door.

Her thoughts were interrupted when she heard the front screen door slam followed by a cheerful bellow.

"Mom, Dad!! We're here! Anyone home?" Allen's voice carried joyfully throughout the foyer. Allyssa dabbed her face and hands with the towel and managed to put on her best smile. After all, she was thrilled to see her babies.

"Oh, in here!" She emerged from the powder room with her arms wide open, ready to embrace her not so little son. Equally happy to see her, Allen wrapped his huge arms around his mother, picking her up and swirling her around. Allyssa squealed with laughter and clung tightly to her youngest. When he finally put her down, she stared up into her handsome son's face.

"My Lord! You've grown another six inches since Thanksgiving! How is that possible?"

"Mother, the way you exaggerate is hilarious! But the way you age, so flawlessly and gracefully is beyond impressive and lacks exaggeration!"

"Well, no one ever accused you of being a liar." Allyssa winked and they laughed at their jokes. "Where's your sister?" As if on cue, Riann stumbled through the door, struggling to manage their luggage.

"Right here. I'd been in sooner if my bighead brother were more of a gentleman and was decent enough to help me with the bags." She finally gave up and let everything drop to the floor. She stepped over them to get to her mother and embraced her as if she hadn't seen her in years. Allyssa reciprocated the love and squeezed her daughter as if she never wanted to let her go.

"Mom," she gasped. "Having a little trouble breathing here."

"Oh, oh…. My goodness! I'm so sorry sweetie. I'm just so happy to see you both! Wow, are you eating in school? You're so thin!"

"Thin! Please! I'll bet I gained ten pounds just from stressing over finals!"

"Well, that's what happens when you try to become a psychologist!" Allen interrupted.

"Dude, not everyone can be a football star." She stabbed her finger into his ticklish side. She loved to tease her little brother. They would do anything for each other. If someone didn't know them, they might believe that they were twins. They could finish each other's thought processes and could tell when the other was troubled or hurting. That's how close they were. Almost simultaneously, they asked,

"Where's dad?" Allyssa tried to hide the annoyance on her face and simply waved her hand.

"He's out back, tinkering around with something back there." She smiled quickly to cover up how she really felt. Both Allen and Riann glanced at each other as they thought her behavior was somewhat strange but thought nothing more of it and darted for the back door. Allyssa's eyes followed behind them as she watched the interaction with her family from the doorway. Randall and Allen hugged and did their father-son secret handshake, chest bump thing that was special to them, and he all but swept Riann off her feet. He gave her a giant poppa bear hug as they called it and kissed her tenderly on her forehead. A long time ago, Allyssa would have marveled at the sight of this, but now this only made her sad. She prayed for God to give her strength to make it through this week so that they could have their last holiday together before the official break-up.

After dinner, they gathered around the fireplace for their traditional cookies, cocoa, and the family game night where they played their all-time favorite games but added a Christmas theme to it. Everything was going well, but Riann would catch the occasional awkwardness between her parents. Once again, she shrugged it off as nothing to be concerned about and went back to having fun. She bit into a freshly baked chocolate chip cookie and said, "This is so delicious mom! The only thing that's missing is some French vanilla ice cream." Everyone agreed, and she went into the kitchen to check the freezer. When she didn't see any in there, she went to the garage to check the deep freezer. As she found what she needed, she headed back inside, but then something in the back seat of Randall's car caught her attention. She stopped in her tracks to investigate what seemed so oddly out of place.

Luggage? Not just an overnight bag, but several suitcases that were neatly arranged across the back seat. Riann took a moment to reflect on the strange behavior from her parents that she had witnessed throughout the evening. She swallowed hard and

grasped at her heart as fear rushed over her feeding her suspicions. She re-entered
the house and paused for a moment again to observe Randall and Allyssa. Sure, the laughter was real while they were interacting with her and her brother, but the tension was thick enough to build a brick wall between her parents.

"Dad, Mom, what's going on?" Her tone was serious, and she tried hard to steady her breathing and to remain calm as she felt her heart was going to explode with anticipation of not knowing what was going to happen next.

Still laughing, Randall began to explain something that Allen had just said, but she cut him off, which made everyone turn to acknowledge her. She was still holding the ice cream that was beginning to defrost in her hand, but the coldness didn't seem to phase her at all. She was growing furious, but she was still fighting to maintain her composure.

"I'm not talking about that! I'm talking about you! What's going on? Dad, why do you have your packed bags in your back
seat? Is your job sending you someplace for Christmas?" Her face began to flush as it

was becoming harder to resist what she already knew was the answer.

"Oh, um… I just got back from a trip, today. Yeah, I just got home before you kids did." Randall attempted to sell his statement by making it sound matter of fact, like but Riann wasn't falling for it. She knew her father was a terrible liar.

"So, if that were true, why didn't you mention it earlier?" She took a deep breath before she made her next statement. "Dad, you and mom have spent a boatload of money on my education as a psychologist. I'd like to think that you're getting your money's worth by me recognizing 'B.S.' when I hear it." Riann said sternly. She was nervous in how she said it because she has never been the type to speak disrespectfully to her father and wasn't sure how he was going to react, but she wasn't a child anymore, and she was ready to stand up to both of them if that's what it took.

Realizing the seriousness of the situation, Allen raised from his seated position on the floor and came and stood behind his sister, letting her know without saying a word, that he had her back. Allyssa and Randall looked at each other for a moment, then Randall straightened his posture on the sofa and threw up his hands in surrender.

"We might as well tell them." He stated, sounding defeated.

"Tell us what?" Allen asked nervously. Allyssa finally broke her silence and said the words that would shred their family.

"Your father and I have been separated since you guys left at Thanksgiving. I've decided that I no longer want to be married, and I'm seeking a divorce at the start of the year." She allowed them a moment to soak in the shock before she continued. "Now that you guys are grown, and able to handle living on your own, I'm going to put the house on the market, and I'm going to get my own place and continue to pursue my interior decorating business, while your father continues to work and do whatever he does in his spare time." She threw her hands in the air as if to say she was done with it. Randall, Riann, and Allen all started speaking at once with their objections. Allyssa merely stood up and raised her hands again to silence everyone, and simply stated,

"It's settled. There's nothing to discuss. My mind is made up, and there is no changing my mind. With that being said, I still want… I still EXPECT this final holiday to be the best one yet. We're still going on our annual last Christmas Dash shopping spree at the mall tomorrow. We're still going to celebrate Christmas Day together as a family, and heck… I'll even throw in New Year's as a bonus. But as of January 2, 2022, the Peterson family as you currently know it will be no more. Make no mistake children, your father and I still love you guys, and we still love each other. We just think we're better off apart than we are together. No one cheated, it's no one's fault. We've just grown apart, and that's the end of it."

"But mom, you can't just…" Both Riann and Allen tried to interject, but Allyssa wasn't hearing it. She turned her back to retire to her bedroom and said as she ascended the staircase,

"I'm going to bed, everyone; I suggest you all get your rest as well. Randall, since our charade of being the perfect couple, has been exposed, you can go ahead and sleep in the guest room. I expect everyone to be at the breakfast table promptly at eight o'clock so that we can head to the mall by ten o'clock a.m. Good night, all!" With that, she disappeared around the corner followed by the sound of her bedroom door closing.

CHAPTER 2

It was Christmas Eve morning, and the family sets out to do what Allyssa Peterson had instructed. They went to the mall to accomplish their last-minute shopping needs. Allyssa, to say the very least was the only one that was happy about it. The rest of the family was just following suit, but was less than enthusiastic about it, and rightfully so. Since they started this last Christmas dash tradition, the plan was to split up, shop, and meet in the food court for lunch. However, this year when Allyssa made her "start your engines"speech and made her usual statement of "Let's go our separate ways and divide and conquer," seemed to ring differently this time. They really would be going their separate ways after this Christmas. Who knew where they would be next year?

Allyssa's words echoed with Allen. While his facial expression remained stoic, his inner thoughts were deeply saddened. His parents' reasoning for breaking up made no sense. Even though he was in his early twenties, he had the impression that their marriage was intact. Of course, he wasn't so delusional to believe that they were perfect, but he never dreamed that they would be separated let alone seeking a divorce. He was very uneasy and was not in the mood to continue shopping. He used to love hearing the music and allowing the ambiance to get him further in the spirit, but now he was just annoyed.

"Way to go, mom. You found a way to ruin my favorite holiday." He thought to himself. He decided to distract himself with his music. He wasn't paying attention as he continued to walk while he was scrolling through his phone and accidentally bumped into another shopper.

"Hey, watch it!" A lady in a green coat snapped at him. Allen apologetically raised his hands and excused himself. She looked him up and down before rolling her eyes and kept going. With that, Allen had had enough and decided to go and wait in the food court for the rest of the family. He wasn't surprised when he saw his sister Riann already sitting at the table poking at her loaded French fries and sparingly sipping at her lemonade.

"I see you finished your shopping early

too." He said grumpily as he sat down, putting his shopping bags on the ground next to her. "Looks like you got a lot of stuff though."

"Don't be too flattered. Most of it is for me. I didn't see the point in going all out like I normally do if we're all going our separate ways." She said, mimicking her mother. Allen understood where she was coming from and continued to sit there listening to his sister vent her frustrations.

Meanwhile, Randall stood over the jewelry counter in one of the department stores. He found a simple necklace that caught his eye. While he was used to spending top dollar for anything that he admired for his wife. There was something about this necklace that seemed appropriate for this time. He truly loved Allyssa and did not want a divorce. He knew there wasn't a chance in changing her mind once it was made up, but he felt compelled to have the clerk take it out of the case so he could examine it closer.

It was a small gold-linked chain with a divided heart charm. One half of the charm said "best", the other said "friend." He knew it sounded corny, but his sentiment was sincere. He asked the clerk to ring it up and gift wrap it for him. When she was done, he looked at his watch and found that it was getting close to lunch, and time to meet up with the family in the food court. On his way out, he saw Allyssa struggling to balance the packages and bags that she had. He went to her and started helping her. She was somewhat surprised at his thoughtfulness and started to decline, but he had already arranged and picked up most of it.

"Thank you, Randall." She said vaguely.

"You don't have to sound so formal, Allyssa. I'm still your husband. I'm capable of being a gentleman. I'm not oblivious. I can recognize when you need help. Not saying that you need a man to rescue you or anything. I know you're a very formidable woman and can handle yourself. I'm just letting you know that even though you don't want me, I'm still here for you."

"See there?" Allyssa stopped in her tracks.

"What?" Randall asked confused.

"That right there. That's what I'm talking about. One minute you're trying to be helpful and supportive and in the next breath, you turn it into it being about you,

107

and you're making me look like the villain in all this!"

"What are you talking about Allyssa?" Randall asked. His voice cracked as his heart was genuinely breaking, yet he was trying not to make a scene.

"You do that all the time!" Allyssa responded also trying to keep her voice down but allowing her frustration to be known. "You want to swoop in like you're the hero and find a way to put me down in the process. We used to be a team, Randall. Now it's like you've become this selfish person that only cares about how you look. It's like you don't give a damn about the contributions that I make. You don't acknowledge me and the things that I do."

"I don't understand you, Allyssa. I just got through commending you, and you're attacking me."

"Forget it. You just don't get it!" Allyssa started off walking again. Randall tried to keep up with her to continue the conversation, but she cut him off. "Let's just get through the rest of this week so we can move on with our lives."

"You're serious? You want to throw away the last twenty-nine years just like that?" Just then, he noticed that she wasn't wearing her wedding ring. Randall was trying hard to fight back tears that were trying to flow, but Allyssa could see his eyes turning red. She didn't know if she wanted to cry too or stand strong and continue to resist.

"It's a bit late for you to act like you care Randall. It's over. I've been begging you for ages, and I just can't do it anymore."

Back in the food court, Allen and Riann continued their conversation. They had been discussing their disappointment in both Allyssa and Randall.

"And what is dad's problem?" Allen asked. "This is not the solid, headstrong, proud man that I've always known. Where's that Michigan man that is quick to tell someone about his humble beginnings, that was dirt poor but managed to be the first to graduate college and make something of himself? Where's that black pride, fighter spirit that he always taught me to have? When he would help train me for football, he'd always say to me, Son, there are two types of men in the world. Ones that talk about action, and the ones that take action. You can talk about fighting for what you believe in, or you can fight for what you believe in. Don't be the latter.

109

Well, I guess he's finally showing us his true colors because he's definitely not fighting for mom! I can't believe him! He's such a..." His voice trailed off as his attention was diverted to a white man shoving stolen items into another shopper's bag.

"Hypocrite." Riann finished his sentence while still poking at her food.

"Hey!" Allen's voice changed. He sounded resentful.

"What? I'm just following your narrative," Riann said, not following what was going on. She looked oddly at her brother, then realized that he wasn't talking to her. He was responding to something he was witnessing as she saw that his attention was on something else. She was trying to see what he was looking at when he suddenly took off running after the shoplifter snatched another person's bag along with the things he had stolen.

"Where are you going? What's happening?" Riann called after him. Still running, he called back after her.

"Stay with our stuff, I'll be right back! Hey! Hey! Somebody stop that guy!" Allen darted off chasing after the shoplifter. His life-long football training kicked in along with his adrenaline as he dodged in and out of the crowd and different obstacles that were standing in the way. Within no time, Allen had caught up with the thief and tackled him to the ground. Shoppers were stunned at the series of events that had taken place and a crowd of people had gathered around them. They were struggling at first, but Allen managed to get the man down and pin him in a position where he couldn't escape.

Some shoppers called for security while the scuffle was happening. Soon afterwards security, along with the lady whose packages had been stolen arrived. Once Allen saw that help was there, he got up while still grabbing hold of the shoplifter. Security saw that Allen was larger than the man he tackled and saw that he was still holding him and drew their guns on him. They shouted for Allen to let the man go and to get on the ground. At the same time, the lady whose packages had been stolen was yelling in the background.

"Yes! That's him, officers! Arrest him! He's the one that stole my bags!" Allen looked hurt and confused as to why the woman was accusing him until he recognized her as the lady he had bumped into earlier. She continued with her accusations by adding extra untrue details, "Yep that's him. I bet he tried to pickpocket me when he bumped into me before!" She egged on while she felt around her coat to see if anything was missing.

"Lady, please! I didn't steal anything from you! I was trying to help you!!"

Another white person in the crowd added to it by telling the security guards that Allen attacked this poor man for no apparent reason. He claimed that Allen just started chasing him and dove on top of him and beat him up trying to steal his Christmas purchases. With all the commotion, Allen was shocked and appalled by the negative attention that was being turned on him. He tried to explain what happened as other people were trying to chime in on what they witnessed.

"Officer, stop trying to arrest me and just listen for a second!" Allen pleaded. "I didn't steal anything! I saw this lady set her bags down beside her, then this guy put some stolen items in it, then picked up her bags and ran out of the store. I was just trying to stop him! Please, sir! You can run the surveillance cameras and see that I'm telling you the truth!" All the while, security was still trying to place Allen in handcuffs. Meanwhile, other security officers were asking the real shoplifter if he was all right and if he wanted to press charges against Allen. Just then the rest of the Petersons' caught up with the crowd. Randall instructed Allyssa and Riann to stay back and to let him handle it.

"Excuse me, please. What is going on here?" He interjected. Security then turned their weapons on him and demanded that he back up and let them get the situation under control.

"What situation? What are you doing to my son? Let him go immediately!" Randall commanded. They continued to ignore him and continued to try to place him under arrest.

"Sir, I'm not going to tell you again! We're detaining you pending an investigation."

"Detaining me for what?? I didn't do anything! You've got the wrong guy! He's the one that was stealing! Why are you assuming that I'm the culprit when I and everyone else in here just saw me yelling for someone to stop that guy! Why would I do that if I was the one trying to get away?! No! No! You're not going to arrest me! I know my rights!"

"Well, if you know your rights, then you should know that you have the right to remain silent. Anything you say, can and will be used against you in a court of law. You have the right to an attorney. If you cannot afford one, one will be appointed to you." The superior security officer continued with the Miranda rights speech, but Allen kept pleading his case. Randall demanded to know what was going on and asked why the perpetrator was not detained.

"Son, son! Just relax. Let me handle this! I'm going to get you out of this, and best believe we're going to sue the hell out of this mall! But relax for now. Let me take care of this!" Randall tried to speak calmly to his son, but Allen wasn't going for it and continued to resist.

"Hell no! You think I'm just going to let them arrest me! I'm innocent! No, get away from me!" He yelled as he yanked away from both officers again. They began to struggle with him, and Allen knocked one of the officer's hands away. He took a defensive stance as six different officers were surrounding him now. Randall, Allyssa, and Riann began yelling over the rest of the crowd, begging for Allen to comply. Everything seemed to go in slow motion as Allen nervously looked around him. His eyes darted desperately from left to right as he tried to assess what to do once they came at him. Before he could complete his thought, his eyes fell on his family, and he managed to make eye contact with each of them as if he were trying to apologize to them individually. Everything seemed to go silent until the next thing you heard was a gunshot! Allen's eyes widened with shock and fear, followed by tears as he stumbled backward towards the right. He had been shot in his shoulder and had stumbled back trying to catch his balance. Another security officer thought he was trying to run away and shot him again, this time in his back! With that Allen flung forward as he fell to the ground and landed on his face. Screams rang out amongst the crowd, and naturally, Allyssa and Riann tried to hurdle over everyone to get to him. It took all the strength that Randall had to hold his wife and daughter back out of fear that they would be shot as well. Their screams pierced the air higher than everyone as people scattered as they tried to get out of the way.

The security officers scrambled quickly to surround Allen and place him in handcuffs, making sure that he didn't have time to recover and continue resisting. While still holding them back, Randall looked at Allen, and frantically called out to him. Allen was still breathing and still able to blink his eyes, but he wasn't saying anything. Randall screamed for him to stay with them, and not to give up. He commanded that he fight to stay alive while all Allen could do in the process was blink to let them know that he understood.

CHAPTER 3

Allen was rushed to the hospital and was undergoing emergency surgery. The media and social media were already blowing up with the events that had happened. Allyssa and Riann held tightly to each other as they watched the news coverage on the television. Someone had used their cell phone to record the scuffle and the shooting. Riann was disgusted that they managed to show the part that made Allen look guilty, but didn't show what led up to that part. The news continued to report "eyewitness" accounts, and of course, most of them were white spectators commenting on what they believed happened.

"We were shopping and having a grand old time when this extra-large black guy tackled this white guy for no apparent reason. I mean, just pulverized him." One white person reported. Another one stated, "Yeah, I've seen how people get upset on Black Friday when someone got the last deal, but this is ridiculous! Violence is never the answer. I just pray this incident doesn't ruin Christmas for the rest of us forever."

"My kids are traumatized! We came here to see Santa! And now, I'm going to have to explain to my kids that the police got the bad guy, and everything is going to be okay now. I just thank God that security was there to protect us! It could have been a lot worse!" Another white woman added along with the fake tears she could drum up.

"OMG!" Riann finally blew up! "Are you listening to this!!! How dare they! Is anyone interested in the truth? Where's the damn news crew! I'm going to tell them what happened myself!" Riann fumed. She paced fiercely back and forth as she continued her rant. She was so angry that she was almost hysterical. "Why aren't they reporting the facts? They're the damn news! I thought it was their job to investigate and report the facts! They report speculation! And where is dad while all this is going on?" She demanded to know. Allyssa took a deep breath before responding to her daughter.

"He's on the phone with his law firm retaining one of the partners for our lawyer." Riann looked at her mother, and was annoyed and belted out, "How can you be so calm? This is your son fighting for his life right now! Don't you even care about what happens to him?"

"Of course, I care!" Allyssa fired back.

"How do you think I feel? I'm scared to death right now! But I must focus my energy on praying that God heals your brother. I can't worry about the Idiocracy of ignorant people that don't know the truth. God will reveal what happened and then they will see that my son is a saint!" Allyssa could no longer maintain her composure. She allowed herself to break down and fell weakly into her chair. Riann instantly felt sorry for her and regretted accusing her mother of such foolishness. Of course, she knew that she cared. What mother wouldn't at this time. Riann went to her mother and hugged and kissed her.

"I'm sorry, mommy. I didn't mean it." She tried her best to comfort her, but Allyssa was a mess. Riann knew that whenever Allyssa was that upset, she needed decaf coffee or a hot cup of tea to calm her down.

"I'm going to get us something to calm our nerves, mom. I'll be right back." She kissed her mother softly on the cheek one last time and squeezed her hand before she left. Riann waited until she was out of sight before she broke down herself. If it weren't

119

for the wall holding her up, she may have fallen straight out on the floor and didn't care who saw her. She held tightly to her own body and imagined that she was holding her little brother.

Being raised in the church, Riann had never really prayed on her own for anything serious. Yes, she prayed for small things that had little relevance like passing a test, or that the cops didn't notice her speeding when she knew she was. But she never had a reason to talk to the Lord about anything. She didn't know what to pray for or how to pray. She knew she wanted her brother to survive and those stupid security guards to pay for what they did to him! Her face grimaced at the thought of how they treated him, but then she sobbed harder at the thought of what a good person her younger brother is and how his football career may be over! She dreaded that thought as she imagined him in a wheelchair for the rest of his life.

"Lord, I don't exactly know the right words to say, but you know my heart and you know what my family stands in need right now. Please, don't take my brother from me. Now that my parents are getting divorced, he's really all I have. I'll do anything, Lord. I'll start paying attention in church services, I'll do more community service, I'll stop talking bad about people, just please spare my brother. Help him to have a great quality of life. Please bring him to a full recovery. Please just save my family. My parents won't survive if you take their son. Just.... please! Amen." She concluded as she didn't know what else to say. She felt so weak as her sobs took over. She allowed herself to sink to a sitting position against the wall. Her head fell into her arms that were clasped around her knees.

A woman passing by saw her in despair. She knelt beside her and whispered soft words of encouragement.

Although Riann never looked up to see the woman, she felt her presence and felt a serenity that wasn't there before.

Once Riann had calmed down, she finally looked up to thank the woman, but she was already gone. Riann rose to her feet and felt at ease like everything was going to be okay.

Back in the hospital waiting room, other patients' families were filtering in and out as their loved one's issues were being addressed. Allyssa felt she had been there for an eternity, although it had only been a couple of hours. She had finally managed to calm herself down enough to where she could sit up straight in the uncomfortable seats the hospital provided. She looked catatonic as she stared off into space getting lost in her thoughts. She had long stopped listening to the nonsense that was being reported on the news. They didn't know her baby. He was not the criminal they were making him out to be. She couldn't wait to sue that mall and every individual security officer there! She gritted her teeth and wrenched her handkerchief at the thought of making them pay for what they had done to her son!

"We're going to own this mall by the time we're through with them!" She thought angrily to herself. "We'll rename it Peterson's Mall… our family portrait will be plastered all over the place." She paused in her thoughts to reflect on that last part. Their family portrait. The words made a heavy thud sound in her heart and mind. She swallowed hard at the thought of the words she stated previously. She felt as she was being haunted by them now as they rang over and over in her ears.

"…As of January 2, 2022, the Peterson family, as you currently know it will be no more! No more! No more!"

The words echoed. "I've decided that I no longer want to be married, and I'm seeking a divorce at the start of the year. We just think we're better off apart than we are together. Better off apart. Let's just get through the rest of this week, so we can move on with our lives. Move on." At that moment, she glanced down at her left hand where her wedding ring used to be. She reflected on the night before when she removed it from her finger and put it in her purse.

"Might as well get used to not wearing it." She had said smugly to herself at the time when she took it off. She hated the way her sarcasm made her feel right now. All the emotions from her fondest memories of their family, watching Allen and Riann growing up, and the tragic events of the day kept swarming and swirling in her mind. Finally, she started to get dizzy and couldn't take it anymore.

Allyssa steadied herself as she rose to her feet. She felt weak and realized it was because her blood sugar was getting low. She hadn't eaten anything since that morning at breakfast which wasn't much considering the awkwardness that she tried to pretend wasn't happening, and she missed lunch for obvious reasons. She decided to see if the cafeteria was open, although she doubted it since it was Christmas Eve. Maybe there was a vending machine somewhere close by that she could get a snack out of. She was fumbling around in her purse looking for loose change when she bumped into a tall white man.

"Oh, I'm so sorry. Please excuse me!" She said nervously. Her hands were shaking, and she shielded her eyes to hide her embarrassment. She didn't want to burst out crying again in front of a stranger, so she held her head down, ashamed and afraid to look him in the eye.

"No worries," he replied kindly. "I should have been watching where I was going. Hell, I'm so wrecked with worry about my daughter, that I wasn't…"

"No," Allyssa cut him off and was finally able to look at him. "It was my fault. I was digging for some change, and I was not paying attention. Are you alright?" She asked, genuinely concerned.

"Yeah, I'm fine." He laughed. "Hell, if a little woman like yourself can hurt a big guy like me, I need to check myself in because that means I'm as weak as a paper leaf!" He laughed at his own joke. Allyssa wasn't sure how to take it, so she smiled halfheartedly and stepped to the side so that he could take a seat. As he moved around her, he took a good gander at her and checked her out. Even though she was wearing a mask, he thought she was very attractive, and he noticed that she wasn't wearing a wedding ring. His eyes widened with the thought that he had a chance with her. It didn't matter to him that she was in a hospital waiting room, obviously very concerned about someone. Clearly, he was there for the same reason. In his twisted way of thinking, he thought that was a perfect circumstance for two people to meet. They already had something in common without even trying.

For a large man, his ego was even larger. He credited that trait to his job as a fireman. He was used to desperate women flinging themselves at him after having saved them from a crisis. He figured that this was no different. He would just have to figure out a way for him to come across as a "rescuer" in this situation. If nothing else, he could always offer a shoulder to cry on. Hell, he might even find it beneficial to need a shoulder to cry on himself. It was too early to tell just yet, but he let the thought linger in the back of his mind for now. Allyssa's words broke his daydreaming as he regained focus on the present.

"Excuse me, Mr…"

"Frazier. Louis Frazier." He extended his hand. Allyssa shook it out of professional habit while she continued, "Mr. Frazier. Would you mind saving that space where I was sitting, please? I need to grab something from the vending machine and splash some water on my face. I'll be right back though."

"Of course. To this day, my momma would have my backside if she felt I was being ungentlemanly like." He was trying his best to impress her. He took off his jacket and laid it gently across the seat she had pointed out where she had been sitting. Allyssa thanked him and disappeared around the corner. Louis felt proud of himself and took a seat near hers.

A short while later, Allyssa returned with her snack of peanut butter crackers and a soda. She thought it was a bit strange how Louis greeted her so warmly as if she had been gone for ages, but she decided to think nothing more of it and find something else to focus on. She had forgotten to plug her cell phone in the night before, so her battery

126

was too low to play a game. Allyssa glanced around the room, looking for something to keep her occupied, but there was nothing to do other than people watching since all the magazines and books were no longer available due to Covid-19 restrictions. She was sick of the news, especially since it was one half-truth story after the other. Frustrated, Allyssa sighed heavily and turned her back towards the television, and propped her arm up over the conjoined seat next to hers. She took another bite of her crackers and crunched softly to herself. She attempted to close her eyes and just meditate, but Louis' voice broke her concentration.

"Are those helping you feel better?" She opened one eye to see if he was speaking to her. When she realized he was addressing her, she swallowed and cleared her throat before responding.

"Yeah, a little. My blood sugar was getting low, I needed something since I didn't get lunch. I'm not hungry now, but it's been a long day, and it feels like it's going to get longer."

"Yeah, I know what you mean." He paused to admire her full beauty since this was his first time seeing her without her mask. She was even prettier than he imagined. He pretended that the back of his ear was aching so that he could take his mask down too. He was actually trying to flaunt his handsome face and million-dollar smile at her to so that she could get a good look at what he hoped she wanted, even if she didn't know it yet. Allyssa was about to close her eyes again, but he re-started the conversation and she felt obligated to listen. She figured it couldn't hurt. She had nothing else to do, and maybe it would help keep her mind off worrying about Allen.

"Hopefully, we won't have to be here too long," He continued. "I mean, how long does it take to wrap a broken arm, huh?"

"How long have you been here?" Allyssa asked just trying to contribute to the conversation, although she really didn't care.

"Since about eleven o'clock this morning. Yeah, we went sledding with our neighbors and she took a nasty spill down the hill. Pretty sure she's got a broken arm, a few scrapes here and there, but I'll tell you what… she took it like a champ. Yep. Sure did. I was proud of my baby girl. No tears or nothing." He grinned with satisfaction with the thought of knowing that he raised such a tough little girl.

"Wow! Poor kid. " She looked at her watch. "It's getting late into the afternoon. They must be busy today. " She looked around the waiting room. While there were a few people there, it seemed they weren't that busy at all. She shrugged and leaned back in her seat again.

"Well, yeah. Either that or they may be short-staffed today. I mean it is Christmas Eve. I'm sure people are enjoying their much-needed time off with their families or somethin'. But um… my Nance. That's my baby. She's eight years old, and boy is she a trooper! She didn't even want me to stay back in the room with her." He laughed and continued. "She says, 'Dad, you go on now! I've got this! If I need ya, I'll text ya!' Then she shooed me away, just like that!" He giggled again as he mimicked her motions.

"Well, she sounds amazing! I certainly pray she feels better soon."

"Oh, Nance? Yeah! She's got this one in the bag. I couldn't be prouder if I had had a son!" He boasted. Just then, he noticed that Allyssa shifted a little in her seat as if she were uncomfortable. "Oh, I'm sorry. Am I talkin' too much? I tend to do that

129

sometimes when I'm nervous, or bored, or both. " He tried to flash his pearly whites again, but Allyssa remained unimpressed.

"Listen, I can just sit here and keep my trap shut if you'd like, Ms. Umm... Hey! I just realized I don't know your name!" He had been trying to figure out a subtle way to ask her name for what seemed like forever now.

"Allyssa." She returned as she moved her hair back away from her face. She took a slow sip of her drink and another bite of her cracker.

"Amazing. We've been sittin' here all this time, and I completely forgot to ask you that. How rude of me. Well, Ms. Allyssa. It's a pleasure to meet you. You look like you could use a cup of coffee or something. Can I treat you to a cup?" He tried to ask as casually as he could without sounding like he was hitting on her in which he was. But Allyssa caught on and thought surely, he wouldn't be so classless as to pick up a woman as if they were at a bar.

"No, but thank you. My daughter is supposed to bring me some back soon." She said, looking around for her. She had noticed that Riann had been gone for a long time and should have been back by now.

"Oh, you have a daughter too. How old is she? If you don't mind me askin'..." He added at the end. Before she answered, Allyssa, scoffed to herself and thought,

"This guy thinks he's slick! He's definitely flirting with me!" She didn't know if she should be disgusted or flattered. She was a little bit of both. She was just about old enough to be his mother. She thought she may be on the market soon, but she was not trying to be a cougar. Gross, who had time for this? She looked at him a little closer.

"She's twenty-four. She's graduating from college soon." She added on purpose to accentuate their age difference hoping it would deter him. "There she is now." She nodded in the direction of the coffee machine that was in the corridor. Louis turned around and saw one of two women that were standing at the hot beverage vending machine. The one he noticed was a slender young white woman with long, thick brown hair similar to Allyssa's.

Genuinely looking surprised, Louis said, "No way. You can't have an adult child!

"Correction, I have two adult children. That's why I'm here. For my son." She allowed her voice to become stern to remind Louis that she was there for him, not to be wooed by the handsome stranger that's supposed to be so concerned for his super trooper tomboyish daughter!

Oblivious to what her intent was, he continued the conversation, as he changed his position in his seat to turn more towards her giving the impression that he was even more intrigued by her now. When he noticed the grimace on her facial expression, he figured he should tone it down a notch or two, so his next approach was to sound more empathetic and sympathetic.

"I'm so sorry. Here I am going on and on about me. I didn't ask you why you're here and how you're feeling. What happened to your son?"

He honestly wanted to know. Allyssa could see that he wasn't going to leave her alone about it, so she simply said, "Some IDIOT at the mall attacked him for no apparent reason!" She squeezed her eyes closed to try to keep from crying again and clenched her fist resisting the urge to punch something. Shocked, Louis dropped his mouth and pointed towards the television.

"That was *your* son that got attacked?" He asked. Allyssa's tears began to flow again, and Louis instinctively got up to console her. He wrapped one arm around the back of her shoulders and used his other hand to gently pat and rub her other shoulder as he tried to comfort her. He didn't mean to upset her. "I'm so sorry. I had no idea. How is he? Is he going to be all right?"

"He's in surgery!" A voice snapped somewhat startling Louis. He was confused to say the very least when he looked up and saw the face of Riann. Without giving him a moment to process, Riann spoke harshly again. "Excuse me, who are you?" She stared sharply at him. She shifted her position as she juggled bags of food and cups of coffee in her hands. Finally, she motioned with her head for him to move over and let her sit and console her mother.

Louis slowly eased away from Allyssa and held up his hands in surrender as if he had gotten busted for a crime he was in the process of committing. Showing no fear, Riann continued to stare him down until he moved a comfortable enough distance away for her satisfaction. She set the bags of food down in another seat, and side hugged her mother for support. Still looking confused

133

to what just happened, and why was this very tanned woman standing there instead of the fair-skinned young lady that he had just seen wasn't there, Louis apologized for overstepping his boundaries.

"Just helpin' is all." His face was beet red as he was embarrassed and bewildered. His eyes scanned the room for the other young lady he had seen. Sure enough, she was sitting with another group of people on the other side of the room. As the realization that Riann was the daughter set in, he felt as though he wanted to vomit. He thought to himself, how could this be her daughter? Was she adopted or something?

"I'm sorry I took so long. I remembered that you didn't eat, and that you probably need to take your medicine, so I went and got you some real food." Allyssa held up her crackers and drink.

"Mom, that's not a meal! You need to eat and keep your strength up. Here, I got you a turkey sandwich and some chicken noodle soup."

After staring at them closely, Louis could see the resemblance. Wow! So, Ms. Allyssa was one of "those white women" he assumed. After thinking several minutes, he had it all figured out. She got with a dead-beat black man that forced her to raise a child on her own! He was willing to forgive her for being with a black man. After all, he had probably manipulated her and used her to get what he wanted then left. At some point she got with a white man and had a son. Who unfortunately got attacked by that thug in the mall earlier that day!

"Black Lives Matter my ass!" He cringed at the thought.

CHAPTER 4

Louis struggled mentally with adjusting to the idea of pursuing a relationship with a woman that had a biracial daughter. All the talk and trouble that would stir up in his immediate circle of family and friends. How would he explain that? He was so deep into his thoughts that he almost didn't hear the doctor that had come out to speak with him. For the second time, the doctor called out,

"I'm looking for the parent or guardian of Nancy Frazier." She said a little louder this time as she searched the waiting room. Louis finally snapped out of his trance and answered.

"Yeah, right here." He stood up to meet her.

"Sir, if you could come with me where we could speak privately." She motioned with her hand to have him step aside. Riann asked her mother about him.

"Who was that guy?"

"Nobody, really, he was keeping me company while you were gone. Girl, he about talked my ear off the whole time, but it was a good distraction. And get this, I think he was flirting with me! I mean, who does that while their sick kid is in the hospital?"

"A creepy person! I don't want you talking to him mom, he looks crazy." Riann said as she glanced over her shoulder, looking in his direction. Allyssa peeked at him as well and agreed with her daughter. She watched his face grow with concern and wondered what the doctor was telling him.

In the corridor outside of the waiting room, the doctor was indeed delivering some concerning news. She explained to Louis that Nancy's broken arm was just the discovery of an even bigger issue that she was having. She was getting more information from Louis about their family history that she felt maybe more relevant to finding their diagnosis.

"Sir, with the symptoms that Nancy has been displaying and that you have been describing to us, we have reason to believe that Nancy may have something called Myelodysplastic Syndrome or MDS for short. Basically, it's a very rare bone marrow disease where the blood cells that the body produces aren't producing them in a sufficient amount and/or abnormally, which causes the blood cells not to mature in the way that they should."

"So, what does this mean for my baby? What do we need to do?" For the first time, Louis showed genuine concern for his child.

"Bottom line, we need to run more tests to confirm it, but it looks like she is going to need a blood transfusion to help her."

"Okay then. Where do I go? I can go give blood right now."

"You are welcome and encouraged to do so. However, it may not necessarily be your blood that saves her."

"Wait, what? Why? I'm her father! That's partially my blood running through her veins!" His face reddened as he raised his voice.

"Your daughter has a rare blood type – AB negative. This means that your blood type is either A, B, or AB negative as well. For someone to have that blood type, it means they received a type A and a type B antigen from both of their parents. Nancy needs a blood donation from either type AB negative or any negative blood type. Someone with an O negative or AB negative would be great, but those are rare blood types. And with being in a pandemic right now, blood resources are scarce for those rare blood types. Finding a match would be very difficult at this time."

Louis smeared his hands over his face as if trying to wipe off the worry. He took a moment to steady himself and lower his voice before he got in the doctor's face. His icy blue eyes were piercing through hers as he lowered his posture to look her eye to eye.

"Are you saying, that it's impossible?"

"Not impossible, sir, just extremely difficult. I just want you to be prepared for…"

"For her to die! Never!" He said through clenched teeth. He rudely pointed his finger in the doctor's face. "You get back there, and you find some blood for my baby. I don't care if you go out of state for it! You save my daughter, you hear?" He stormed off to go outside to catch his breath. Louis and Randall caught eyes briefly as they passed each other in the hallway. Each thought nothing of the other and continued to step to their destinations.

Randall entered the waiting room and stood with his hands on his hips as he searched for his family. He was physically and emotionally drained, but he continued to hold it together for the sake of his wife and daughter's support. He finally found where they were seated and marched over toward them.

"Any news?" He asked, still standing in front of them. Riann jumped up and flung her arms around her father's neck. He embraced her as well, then gently held her face as he looked her over, making sure she wasn't injured in any way.

"Where have you been?" Both Allyssa and Riann asked simultaneously. Randall explained that he had been getting all the investigation information from the security officers at the mall. He spoke with the police about the events that took place and filled his partners in at the law firm about it all. He was also trying to find out what happened to the initial shoplifter, who managed to slip away during the commotion when everyone was screaming and running during the shooting.

"So, any word on how Allen's doing?" He said, finally sitting down on the other side of Allyssa. He instinctively wrapped one arm around her shoulder the same way Louis had earlier. He pressed his head against hers and kissed the side of her hair. He whispered in her ear that everything was going to be okay and that he loved her very much. Allyssa closed her eyes and absorbed his words that meant so much at that moment. She connected her hand with his that was across her shoulder and squeezed it tightly.

"He's still in surgery. All we know is that doctors are doing all they can."

"Good. And in the meantime, I gave blood." Randall added.

"That's a good idea daddy, I think I will too." Riann chimed in. Randall told Riann where to go to give blood and she left to take care of that. Once she was gone, Randall cupped Allyssa's face within his hands and looked her deeply in the eyes. She placed her hands on top of his and allowed herself to melt.

"I can't lose my baby, Randall, I just can't." She sobbed into his shoulder.

"You won't. I promise. Our baby is going to make it." He held his wife tightly, trying to make sure that she felt secure, and for a moment she did. The news was on again, and this time the person that spoke up was black. Both Randall and Allyssa sat up to hear what they had to say.

"All I know is, dude was chasing the white man and was yelling for someone to stop him. Then he dove on the guy and was holding him down. When security got there, they pulled guns on him, and he kept saying they had the wrong guy, but nobody wanted to listen. The next thing you know, security shoots him." She started getting emotional.

"I'm just tryna figure out, why they had to shoot him like that. All they had to do was listen! I'm not sayin' that he is innocent, cause I wasn't there to see how it jumped off. I'm just tryna make it make sense, ya' know. " She started wiping away her tears before the news crew cut away from her.

"See that!" Randall said, getting upset.

"See what the media does to us? They let all these white people say whatever they want to make Allen the bad guy that deserves to get shot! But when someone black gets on here makes you think about it, they instantly want to cut away from the truth because they don't want people to know the truth!" He was fuming.

"Why didn't *you* go on television and give the truth about our son?" Allyssa asked, getting upset again. "They don't know how he's been an honor student his whole life. They don't know that he's in college and cares about his community! They don't know what a wonderful person he is! You did all this 'handling it', but you didn't get on TV to clear our son's name! Where are the cameras? Where's the news crew? I'll get on there and tell them if you won't." She scoffed. "I don't know why I expected differently from you! Like I've always said, you're not here, even when you are here!" Allyssa started snatching up her purse and gathering her things.

"Wait just a damn minute!" Randall stood up after her. He grabbed hold of her arm to stop her from walking away and made her turn to face him. "I'm getting sick of you blaming me for everything and nothing at the same time! What exactly do you want from me, Allyssa? I'm doing the best I can for this family, and somehow, I'm in the wrong no matter what I do. You're making me out to be this horrible husband that's not there for his family. The truth of the matter is you're making excuses not to be with me anymore. What's really going on with you? Are you seeing someone else?" Randall glared at her with fire in his eyes. As if the timing couldn't have been worse, Louis comes back in and sees their heated exchange in the hallway.

"Hey!" He yelled out and gained

attention from everyone. "Hey, you! What do you think you're doing to her?"

Randall rolled his eyes at the nosey white man and temporarily ignored him. He continued speaking to Allyssa.

"Are you going to answer me?" Before Allyssa could answer him, Louis stepped in between them and scooted Allyssa back as if to get her out of harm's way.

"Maybe you didn't hear me, boy, I'm sayin' back away from her."

"Boy!" Randall said, finally facing Louis and squaring up his posture, as he stepped closer to his face, "Who the hell are you calling boy?"

"Allyssa, are you okay? Do you want me to get rid of this guy? Being confused about what was going on herself, Allyssa had trouble finding words to say to either of them. Randall interrupted anyway by saying,

"Oh yeah, right. I get it. White woman sheds some tears, and immediately you assume I'm hurting her! Hold up, he called you by your first name. Why does he know your first name? Is this your man or something?"

"Or something," Louis interjected.

"Hey, this is a private matter between my wife and me!"

"Your wife?" Louis was confused and whipped his head to face her.

"Yes! MY WIFE! Who the hell are you?" Randall asked, getting even closer to his face.

"Looks like I'm your worst nightmare!" Louis said, stepping close enough to Randall that they were almost touching noses. Allyssa finally stepped between them. She looked like a mouse between two mountains. However, her voice was loud and clear.

"ENOUGH! BOTH OF YOU!" They both looked down at her then back to each other. Allyssa used both her arms to separate them. Her arms felt like spaghetti noodles, but she was managing to hold them at bay. She turned to Louis first.

"It's okay Louis. This is my husband. He's not going to hurt me. We're just having a disagreement that's all."

"Yeah, right. That's what all you women like to say until he beats you to a bloody pulp. Listen, it's okay. I've got your back. I'm not going to let him hurt you. You're safe with me sweetheart."

"SWEETHEART?" Both Allyssa and Randall asked.

"Allyssa, is this why you want to divorce me?" Randall asked, hurt.

"NO! Of course not. I just met him today!" She turned back to Louis. "I swear I'm fine. He's not the abusive type! Please just go away. It's not what you think. I can handle this!"

"You heard MY wife. GO AWAY! ARE YOU DEAF? STEP BRUH! WHY YOU STILL STANDING HERE LIKE YOU WANT SOME OF THIS?!" Randall was loud and beyond heated at this point. For the second time in the same day, racial profiling would rear its ugly head. To add insult to injury, Allyssa had him looking like the thug people would believe him to be since he was ready to throw blows! He hadn't been in a fight since college, and he was angry with himself for losing his cool. He had to remember that this wasn't the way to behave. Especially right now with his son upstairs literally fighting for his life.
What would it look like if he got arrested right now? He paced back and forth for a moment to regain his composure.

"Hey, I've got nothin' to lose. I'm standing here. I'll have you know, I'm a black belt and a firefighter!" Louis egged on. Randall didn't back down on his smack talk even though he was still pacing trying to calm down.

"Am I supposed to be scared because you have a black belt? That means nothing to me! I'll take that little black belt of yours and whoop you with it!"

"Both of you please! Stop it! I can't deal with this! Louis! Go away. I need to talk to my husband." Allyssa pleaded. Louis walked away. Allyssa turned to face Randall. She was pale and grief-stricken. She looked as though she aged ten years in ten minutes.

"Randall, how dare you believe I'm having an affair?"

"You tell me! You have this random Rambo-looking ass fool ready to get his ass beat over you! You want this divorce without really giving a reason why. You just decided that you no longer love me, and I'm supposed to be okay with that? I love you damn it! I love our kids, and I don't want a divorce! And if it means that I must fight for you to believe that then that's what I'm going to do!"

Allyssa was speechless. What if he was just saying that in the heat of the moment? What if once things got back to "normal" he would just go back to ignoring her and being

147

involved in his work? She decided to keep her thoughts to herself for now and let the situation die down. Just then, they heard a call for a code blue. Staff members from all over dropped what they were doing and proceeded to a room.

For a moment, Randall and Allyssa were afraid that it was Allen. They held onto each other. Louis also was concerned that it may be his daughter and stood up to see where everyone was headed. Fortunately for all of them, the code wasn't for either of their loved ones. They caught eyes for a moment as each of them breathed a sigh of relief and was glad to see that it wasn't for the other person either. They nodded silently at each other and went back to their seats.

"I need some fresh air," Allyssa said.

"I'll come with you," Randall said, reaching for his coat.

"No, thank you. I need to be alone for a minute." Not wanting to cause another scene, Randall backed off and let his wife walk away. His heart was heavy. He wondered what he was going to do. He needed to go for a walk himself and just picked a direction at random and started walking. He wandered around until he found

148

himself at the door of the chapel. He felt an overwhelming feeling to go inside.

CHAPTER 5

After Allyssa had taken some time to herself, she re-entered the hospital. As she was walking back to the waiting room, she saw Louis posted up in the corner. His once icy blue eyes were now bloodshot as he had been crying. She couldn't help but stop to ask what was wrong. She glanced over her shoulder to make sure that Randall or Riann couldn't see her as she didn't want them to get the wrong idea.

"My baby girl is in desperate need of a blood transfusion. They're looking for a match. It's going to take a miracle. I just came from sitting with her. She barely even knew I was there. She looks so weak and pale. I feel so hopeless. I'm used to being her hero, and right now, my blood can't even save her." He sobbed harder but then turned his face away towards the wall. Allyssa didn't know what to say other than not to worry and that she was sure they would find a blood donor soon. She patted his back to comfort him. Louis wiped his face and turned back to face her. His demeanor was different as he positioned himself to ask his next question.

"Is your son white or black?"

"What? What does that have to do with anything?" Allyssa asked, appalled that he would go there.

"Please just tell me, I need to know. Because you said, your son was attacked by that thug in the mall."

"No! I never said that! I said, my son, was attacked by an idiot at the mall!"

"So, your son was the one that was shot, not the one that was tackled."

"I still don't see what relevance that has!" Allyssa fired back.

"It's relevant because that means your son is black too!"

"My son is biracial if you must know! But what does his race have to do with him fighting for his life?" Allyssa was becoming furious.

"I'm just trying to understand why a fine woman like yourself would get with a black man that doesn't take care of you the way that he should? I mean, what did you see in him?"

"For starters, it wasn't the color of his skin! I met and fell in love with my husband because of who he is! Not because of where he came from. My husband is a gentleman and a scholar! His parents raised him to care about himself, and others in his community. They put him through college. He's a lover of Christ and a provider for his family. He's a giver, and would rather starve himself than to see someone else go hungry! My husband stands up for what he believes in. He teaches the youth to speak up for the underdogs in this world, which is what happened at the mall today. My son saw a WHITE MAN, stealing from someone else, and tried to stop him! Then he was wrongfully accused and shot twice because security assumed he was guilty when they saw his skin and not sin! And for the record, my husband being black is not a fault, it's a badge of honor and a bonus! Something, you'll never have!"

Allyssa, Riann, and Randall met up at their seating area around the same time. Allyssa was still fuming from the heated discussion she had just had, while Randall was excited. They both wanted to share their news, but Riann beat them to it first.

"There you guys are! I've been looking all over for you! The doctor wants to see us!" They immediately ran back to a private room where a surgeon was waiting.

"We have successfully removed the bullets from Allen's

shoulder and back. The bullet that entered through his back came dangerously close to his spine. We're not sure if he will be able to walk again. The next twenty-four to forty-eight hours will be very critical. We will know more once the considerable swelling has gone down. He's still in a lot of pain, and we've given him some medications to make him comfortable."

"Will we be able to see him?"

"Briefly, he really needs his rest, though. You can talk to him, but he won't be able to respond right now because he is sedated. The best thing is to let him rest. The poor guy has been fighting for hours, and he's going to need all the strength he can get."

"Doctor, will he be himself?" Allyssa asked, looking broken-hearted.

"Prayer is always a good thing. It is Christmas after all, and Lord knows we could use some miracles." The doctor was wearing a face mask, but the Peterson's could tell that he gave a faint, hopeful smile. The doctor closed the door on his way out, leaving the family on their own.

Riann went first to speak to Allen. She rushed through her words of encouragement as she hated to see her baby brother lying unconscious. This was nothing like the time when he was younger and had his tonsils taken out. At least then he was able to interact with her. Now he was in a medically induced coma. Riann couldn't bear the thought of him never waking up. She covered her face before she left his room, as she didn't want her mother to see her crying.

Allyssa took her turn next. She pulled up a stool that was on the side of the bed and held Allen's hand. Although his hand was twice the size of hers, when she looked down at it, all she could see was his baby hand inside of hers. She pulled his hand close to her heart and stroked the side of his face and used her fingers to comb the top of his head where a few hairs were out of place. She sang his favorite Christmas song, 'The First Noel' when she finished, she kissed him softly on his cheek and whispered in his ear, "I love you to infinity and back." With that, she rose stiffly, and she too wiped her tears before exiting his room.

Randall entered last. He stood at the foot of the bed. He wanted to see his son from the top of his head to the soles of his feet. Unbeknownst to anyone else, when he took a walk, he found himself drawn to the chapel. Once inside, he poured out his soul to this random woman, and she told him exactly what to do with their son.

Now that Randall was in position, he proceeded to do as he was instructed. He pulled out a bottle of anointing oil from his pocket and poured some on the palms of his hands. He opened his arms, and outstretched them to heaven and began to give God glory and praise. From there, he laid hands on the places where Allen was shot and prayed that his son would be stronger and better than before, and that God anointed and appointed him to glory where God would truly be honored! When Randall finished, he kissed his oiled finger before drawing a cross on Allen's forehead. He whispered, "I love you, and may God bless you and keep you, son." Then quietly left his room.

Hours later, the Peterson's were huddled together in their spot in the waiting room. Riann had made herself comfortable by using Randall's leg as a pillow as she stretched out across the empty seats next to her. Allyssa used Randall's chest as her pillow as his arms embraced them both. He had fallen asleep himself and had rested his head against the wall. Allyssa's neck was beginning to get sore, so she decided to get up and stretch her legs. Seeing her husband and daughter that way made her remember what times were like when they were younger and happier.

"Lord. What happened to my family?" That's it. She needed to pray just like the doctor said hours earlier. She had been praying the whole time for Allen's recovery, but she needed to get away from all the distractions and go pray for real.

As she went into the chapel, she saw another woman inside. Allyssa apologized and said that she would come back later. The other woman insisted that Allyssa join her. She said that she could use more prayer and offered to pray with Allyssa for her situation. Allyssa really wanted to be alone, but something about her was comforting and inviting. Allyssa took a seat next to the woman being careful to remain socially distanced. The woman could tell that Allyssa was a little uneasy, and didn't know what to expect, so she broke the ice for her.

"Sweet child, you don't need to be uncomfortable. This is a safe place. People come here for prayer, and I'm always here for them. Tell me, what brings you to the hospital today?" The woman's soft and gentle words helped Allyssa to relax. She explained what had happened earlier in the day. The woman asked if she could pray with Allyssa by joining hands with her. She agreed, and the lady placed one hand on Allyssa's shoulder and the other on Allyssa's folded hands.

What amazed Allyssa the most was *the magnificent power* she felt light up the room while she prayed and prophesied over Allyssa's life! Once they finished praying, Allyssa felt an incredible peace rush over her. She no longer felt dismayed or disheartened. In fact, Allyssa urgently needed to make amends with Randall. Before leaving the chapel, she asked the lady her name. She simply responded, "Angel."

Allyssa smiled sincerely at her and commented on how appropriate that was considering she was God sent. Angel laughed and said, "I get that all the time." She waved back. Allyssa was halfway down the hall before she realized that she didn't ask Angel what she needed prayer for. She headed back to the chapel, but once she got there, Angel was already gone.

"That was weird." She thought to herself.

"How could she have disappeared that fast?" She looked around, but didn't see any possible way she could have gotten out of there so quickly. She decided to let it go and rushed back to her family.

When she got back to the waiting room, she was surprised to see the remaining people in the waiting room gathered in front of the television watching the eleven o'clock news. Allyssa joined them as the crowd grew quiet as they awaited the breaking news. The reporter spoke sternly,

"Police are still investigating the case surrounding the shooting at the mall earlier this morning. While it is unclear what happened before, security footage shows this man running with bags in his hands, and then Peterson appearing to call out after him before the chase ensues, while the other man tries frantically to get away. Next, Peterson lunges at the now suspected shoplifter and holds him down while awaiting mall security that would ultimately shoot him while trying to evade arrest. A spokesperson for the family had this to say…

"Allen Peterson is not a criminal. What's criminal are the actions that were taken against him today. When is our society going to learn, that **not** every man with brown skin is dangerous? This situation didn't have to result in violence. Allen Randall Peterson is a model American male. He's an honor student and has a real chance of making it to the NFL. That is until mall security and 'The Karens' at the mall today singled him out as the perpetrator before hearing his side of the story. It's sad to see that while my son, is fighting for his life, the real criminal managed to get away with stolen merchandise and some woman's personal belongings all because they saw a large, darker-skinned man, and chose to be threatened by it, rather than hearing the words of truth!" The speech ended, then the reporter's voice continued, "Police need your help in identifying this man seen in the footage as he is wanted for questioning. Anyone with knowledge of this individual's identity or his whereabouts is encouraged to contact the local police department. In other news..." The reporter's voice faded out amongst the stir in the crowd.

Riann leaped for joy and once again wrapped her arms around her father's neck. Randall, being the humble man that he is, just stood there and nodded, as he was pleased with the news coverage of the updated story. The news interview clearly

159

showed him still in front of the mall, so he had already made the statement before Allyssa accused him of not being there for their family. Allyssa was speechless and felt terrible for the harsh words she had spoken earlier. She just wrapped her arms around her husband and buried her head into his chest. Randall said nothing as well, he just held tightly to his wife and kissed the top of her head.

"Wow! Notice how they were so pleasant in calling the real thief an individual? They've been painting the picture that the black guy was guilty all day long, and then when the truth comes out, the white guy is just an individual, wanted for questioning." Someone in the crowd mocked the news reporter.

"Exactly! Stop being so quick to be the judge and the jury and take time to make it make sense!" Someone else in the crowd said. "I knew it couldn't have been as cut and dry as they were making it sound!"

"I'm just glad it didn't turn into some type of riot and looting!" A different white woman expressed. At that point, everyone spoke up and started arguing with each other.

"See! See there! That's that prejudice we

face all the time! And people have the nerve to wonder why we get upset! For your information, lady, not ALL black people believe in rioting and looting! Some of us believe that rioting is the worst thing you can do!"

"Oh yeah? Tell that to the communities that got burned and smashed up during the riots last summer!" Someone shouted.

"Wow! So, you don't see why we're so angry? Police officers can just keep getting away with murdering and shooting innocent black people, and you don't find that just a bit frustrating?" The original black man that spoke up said.

"I'm not sayin' that, young brother. I completely understand why we're angry. We have every right to be. But tearing up the city because you're upset is not the way to solve the problem. If anything, you make it worse on the community because funds that could have been better spent on things needed to improve local government are now being spent to clean up what was destroyed, further keeping 'us' down."

"Well, how else do you bring awareness to the problem? We're angry! We're tired of being killed for trying to live our day-to-day lives without some 'Karen' or 'Ken' disrupting what we have every right to do!"

"Not by burning it to the ground, I can tell you that much right now!" Someone white said.

"True, I agree with you there. You fight back by boycotting and making sure you vote for your local government official leaders. Establish some type of accountability for when police display such misconduct. Let them know that just because they have a badge, doesn't make them above the law! Now, don't get me wrong, I'm not sayin' all cops are bad cops. I believe most of them out there are good ones. But, the bad ones need to be exposed and dealt with so that trust can be rebuilt within the community," Randall said.

"I don't give a damn about nothin' y'all sayin', man. I say to hell with all that. They don't care about us, so why should we care about them right? Black Lives Matter!"

"All lives matter!" Someone else chimed in.

"I'm so sick of people sayin' that every time someone says, Black Lives Matter! Of course, all lives matter! We never said they didn't! To say that all lives matter is obvious! That's why God put all lives here on earth! No race is superior to the other! But when black lives are being disproportionately exterminated by the blue lives that are supposed to protect all lives, then there lies the problem that clearly all lives don't matter!" Riann fired back.

"Exactly! And don't think that white people weren't out there too, doing just as much looting and rioting! Not only that, why is it that when white people tear up a city they're called patriots, or a rowdy crowd? But when we do it, we're criminals, thugs, and miscreants! It's a double standard."

"Hey! We're just passionate about what we believe in!" The original white man said.

"And we're not?" Someone black asked.

"Well, we're not the ones stealing."

"Need I remind you that this whole shooting today, started with the white guy who stole stuff and tried to get away until the brother stepped in? So, if this had turned into a riot at the mall, it would have been because of the white guy first." Randall added to the conversation. Just then, the original black man that spoke up recognized Randall.

"Yo! You the dude that was just on the news!" The gentleman said, pointing at

Randall. "Way to go, man! Thank you for being a spokesperson, not just for your son, but to our people!" Randall simply held up his hand as a thank you.

"How is your son doing?" Another person asked sincerely. "We're praying for him!"

"Thank you. He's recovering, and we'll know more soon hopefully."

"What a load of crap!" A loud voice came out of nowhere. Everyone turned to see who was rude enough to say that. Another white man said, "If the boy was so innocent, why did he resist then?

Riann spoke up. "Because he just didn't want to be arrested for something he didn't do! All he wanted was for people to listen to him! Which no one was!"

"For all we know, he could have been in co-hoots with that other kid." A white woman added trying to sound relevant.

"Well, I do know, lady because I was there! He saw injustice happening, and he intervened!" Allyssa was getting in their faces. Randall came forward and stood in front of his wife.

"Back up baby, you don't have to listen to these ignorant people who don't know us or our son. We'll have our day in court.

"Just like a coward, going to leave your woman to do all the fighting for you huh?" Louis belted out. He had gotten tipsy after Allyssa tore into him earlier.

"Now wait a minute, Cowboy Bob! What you not fixin' to do is come in here and disrespect my homeboy like that. You caused enough drama in here today. In fact, where's security for this idiot!"

"Hey! I got your damn idiot!" Louis was staggering forward. Just when everyone was starting to meet in the middle and voices were beginning to get heated, but then a loud voice carried out over the crowd that caught everyone's attention!

"You all should be ashamed of yourselves fighting like this on Christmas Eve! All of you are here for the love and support of someone you care about, and this is how you behave? Where is the love? This season is supposed to be about celebrating Christ, who was born for all our sins! Without whom, we'd all be in danger of going to hell! Now, have a seat before I really get angry!" The shortest nurse in the building belted out. At first, the men started to give her lip, but once they saw the much larger security officers line up behind her, they simmered down and took a seat as she commanded.

"Mr. Frazier, I need to have a word with you, please." She continued once everyone settled down.

"Looks like someone did some extra praying for you. While you were over there being all hateful and ungrateful, the Lord decided to bless your baby. We found a match for her blood type. She'll be eligible for the blood transfusion within a few days. Thanks to someone's unselfish ways, your precious daughter is going to be fine."

"Well, that's great! What are we waiting for?"

"Technically, I'm not supposed to tell you this, and I'll deny that I said anything. But your daughter owes her life to that gentleman right over there." She nodded at Randall Peterson. Louis' eyes widened like a deer caught in headlights.

"Umm, hmm. You owe that man a huge apology and a world of thanks! So, while you're so quick to believe that black lives don't matter, I'll bet you change your mind now because if it weren't for his life, your daughter's life would be non-existent by the end of the week. Just thought you should know that." With that, she waved for Mr.

Frazier to follow her back to his daughter's room. Louis stared in disbelief at Randall Peterson. He was at a loss for words. He was humbled and embarrassed at the same time. He was ashamed of himself and vowed to make up for it somehow.

CHAPTER 6

At midnight, the Petersons decided to head home to get some rest. They dreaded leaving, but they knew that the next couple of days were going to be tough, and they needed their strength to make it through. Once they got home, Riann said good night and headed to her room. Allyssa grabbed Randall by both his hands and rubbed them tenderly across the top with her thumbs. She had so much that she wanted to say but couldn't find the words to start. Randall understood what she was feeling, told her to think carefully about what she wanted to say and save it for the morning.

"Are you coming to bed?" She asked. Randall nodded and said that he was going to lock up first. Allyssa took her time letting go of his hand before finally going upstairs. Randall took a long look around the house he used to call home. At first, Randall reminisced about where they spent time as a family when the kids were growing up. He touched the dent in the wall where Allen had been roller skating in the house and tripped trying to stop when he got caught. Then he glanced over to the stairwell where Riann would pose as she pretended to be Juliet waiting for Romeo. From there, he stared at the fireplace where he and Allyssa would sit in front of drinking wine from each other's glass while linked arm in arm.

Then Randall finally noticed the improvements Alyssa had made. He admired the way she had refurbished an old workbench and turned it into a beautiful coffee table. She had even taken the time to repurpose old paint cans and creatively turned them into hanging plants. She had an amazing way of taking the old and ugly things and seeing the potential to make them into something beautiful. After he thought about it, that was pretty much the way she had done him when they met. He had always been the type to believe that there was no such thing as love at first sight, but when he met her, he knew that he wanted to spend the rest of his life with her.

After locking up, he prayed over every inch of the home until he ended up in the guest room. He thanked God for allowing him to be in the house one more time. He figured he may not be in the master bedroom yet, but at least he was under the same roof, which was a good start for him. He had just finished praying when he heard a soft knock at the door. He was surprised to see Allyssa and stepped aside so that she could enter.

"I know you said to wait until morning, but this couldn't wait. I've had a lot of time to think about this, and I realize how selfish I was. I accused you of not being here for our family and ignoring me. I understand now how stupid I've been."

"You're not being stupid," Randall interjected, but Allyssa cut him off again by saying,

"No, really, I was being stupid. I spoke to a lady named Angel in the chapel. And she helped me realize what a terrible mistake I was making."

"You spoke to her too?" Randall asked, intrigued. "What did she say to you?" He sat on the edge of the bed and gave Allyssa his full undivided attention. She stood in front of him as she continued.

"It wasn't what she said exactly. It was the peace I got from my interaction with her. Babe, I could swear that I felt God in the room with us! It was like I got a revelation at that moment that everything was going to be okay. Randall, I don't want us to break up. I want us to keep trying. I know that you are there for us. You've proven that. I can't

believe what a jerk I've been." She held out her hands for him to take them while she desperately searched his eyes
to see if she was coming through to him. Instinctively, Randall received her hands and interlocked them with his. He slowly pulled her closer to him until they were eye to eye. Randall ran his fingers through Allyssa's hair, absorbing all her beauty. He let his hands rest on her shoulders and caressed them gently.

"Sweetheart, I've missed you more than you could ever know." His words were soft yet precise. "I know that we have a lot of work to do. I know it's not going to get back to normal overnight. But I want you and need you to know that I'm in this with you. I'm going to make every effort to prove to you that I'm still in love with you, and I am here for you." With that, he rose from the bed and reached into his pants pocket, and pulled out the small, gift-wrapped box he had gotten from the mall.

"Open it." Randall smiled tenderly. Allyssa accepted the gift and sat on the edge of the bed. Randall sat next to her but watched her face while she opened the gift.

"What's this?" Allyssa didn't want to seem unappreciative, but she was confused when she saw the half of heart-shaped charmed with the word "best" on it. Randall picked up the charm and then turned to face her while getting on one knee the same way he did when he originally proposed marriage to her.

"It's you." He started. "You are the best part of my life. You're my best friend, the best partner, the best mother, best love I've ever known. Even though you wanted to divorce me, I still wanted you to know that I thought of you as simply the best of everything. You have always been my better half, even when I was being too stupid to notice. I'm so sorry for making you feel that I was neglecting you. I spent so much time trying to give you and the kids all the things I never had, that I forgot that what you needed most was me.

I hear you honey, and I want to spend as much time as needed to make sure that you never feel that way again. Allyssa, will you please continue to be what makes the best part of me?"

She grabbed hold of his hands and helped him to his standing position. Randall towered over her, and for the first time in a very long time, they were spiritually on the same level. Allyssa tugged at his shirt to pull him closer to her and met him with the most passionate kiss she could give. It didn't take long for Randall's passion to match hers as he pulled her closer to him and picked her up to carry her to the bed.

Daylight began to peer through the edges of the shades shining on Randall's face, waking him up first, then Allyssa. They smiled lovingly at each other and greeted one another. Allyssa was just about to say that she'd better head back to her bedroom before Riann woke up when there was a subtle knock on the door. Riann's voice was on the other side as she asked if he had seen Allyssa.

"Yep!" He chuckled, then invited her in. Allyssa shot him a dirty look, then smirked as she moved down under the comforter allowing only her nose and eyes to be seen. She wasn't sure why she was so embarrassed. It wasn't like this was the first time one of the kids had come in the room after she and Randall had expressed their love for each other.

"Ma!" Riann said shockingly.

"Hi, sweetie." Allyssa waved from under the covers as she tried to mask her embarrassment. Riann just stood there looking at both of them in shock. Allyssa's face was strawberry red, and Randall wrapped his arm around Allyssa a he smiled proudly. Riann finally spoke out.

"No! Don't tell me anything!" She said as she shielded her eyes. She turned to walk out. "I don't know whether to be grossed out or happy for you. I am, however, more confused than ever! Thanks a lot!" She scurried out of the room. After a couple of seconds, she blurted out, "I'm deciding this is a good thing?" She asked hopefully. Randall and Allyssa answered simultaneously,

"Yes!" They looked at each other and kissed tenderly. On the other side of the door, Riann was trying to shake the image she had just seen but was also relieved that they both seemed happy. She never wanted to see her parents get divorced and was glad to see them trying to work out their differences. She held up prayer hands to the sky and mouthed thank you to God for answering at least one of her prayers.

CHAPTER 7

A short while later, they arrived at the hospital. As they parked and began their walk up the sidewalk, they could see firefighters standing outside with donation buckets and signs. At first, they thought nothing of it, but they were reading the signs as they approached the entryway. Some signs read, **"Stop Racial Profiling!" "An Injustice on One of Us Is an Injustice on All of Us!" "Ask Before Reacting"** They slowly realized that they were raising money for Allen. As they entered the hospital doors, they were most surprised to see Louis Frazier leading the team!

Randall's first reaction when he saw Louis was one of skepticism. He thought he may have been playing a cruel trick and started to get defensive. He stretched out his arms and asked if Louis was trying to come for his family.

"Nah, man. It's not like that." Louis said calmly and sincerely. Once Randall was able to read his demeanor, he lowered his arms slightly to hear him out. Allyssa and Riann joined him on either side, symbolically showing that they stood together in solidarity and as a family. Louis continued,

"This is hard to admit, but I owe you an apology, sir. I should have never made assumptions about your son. I sincerely hope that he's going to be okay. I brought my team here with me to help raise money for his hospital care to show that we care."
Randall's pride took over and cut Louis off.
"You didn't have to do that. I can pay for my son's medical care."
Louis continued.

"I'm not implying that you can't. This is just a way for me to give back and admit where I need help in seein' what's real in this world. I allowed my prejudice to cloud my vision and I was wrong for that. Enough people have the wrong idea about your son, and this is my way of sayin' that I'm not gonna be one of 'em anymore." Allyssa grabbed Randall's hand and stroked his arm. She smiled at him and then at Louis.

"Thank you, Louis. That's very kind of you." Randall hesitated as his pride was still wanting to decline his offer. Louis could tell he was struggling with that, so he reached into his pocket and pulled a wad of cash and placed it directly in Randall's hand while giving him a solid handshake and looked him square in his eyes.

"From the bottom of my heart, I'm truly sorry for what y'all going through." With that, he gave Randall a pat on his shoulder and stepped away to return to his team. Randall finally thanked him for his generosity. Louis simply nodded and walked away.

The Petersons' proceeded inside the hospital and stopped at the nurse's station beforehand to ask about Allen's progress. The latest update was that he had made very little improvement, and they still needed to monitor him to see if the swelling near his spine would go down. The family gathered around his bed, and each took a turn speaking to him, feeding him words of encouragement, and letting Allen know that they were there with him and for him. Then they began to speak to each other.

Riann started first. "So, try not to give me too many details, but what the heck happened after I went to bed last night?" Allyssa and Randall clasped hands and explained that they were staying together. After hearing their story, Riann started to cry. Randall and Allyssa looked at each other as they weren't sure how to respond.

"I'm happy for you guys. I'm glad that you're not breaking up. What still concerns me is whether this is real or not. I mean just two days ago you were dead set on getting divorced. Now, you are love birds again acting like newlyweds. Sometimes, people bond over a traumatic experience, and then later, find out that they really can't stand one another. Are you guys sure about this?" She asked sincerely.

"Baby girl," Randall stated, "Sometimes it takes a near loss to realize what you have. Your mother and I never wanted things to get this bad between us. And what happened to Allen was the wake-up call we needed to put things into perspective. For the first time in ages, we are aware of what the other needs. Which reminds me." He paused for a moment before continuing. "My firm agreed to give me as much time off as I needed. I'm going to be here for all of you."

"Okay, that's cool for now, Dad, but what happens when you go back to work?"

"You didn't let me finish. I've also worked it out with my firm that once I return to work, I'm only working Monday thru Friday. Period. The weekends are reserved for my family and whatever I want to do. Also, I'm taking a vacation every quarter.

I'm taking my wife wherever she wants to go. No work allowed for me!"

"Sweetheart, are you sure?" Allyssa asked.

"Positive." He responded. "And to prove it, they're preparing a contract for me that stipulates everything. I'm a new man, guys. I promise." Riann was satisfied with his answer and wiped her tears away.

"What's going on?" A scratchy voice came from nowhere. The Petersons' looked around at each other as if trying to figure out where the voice came from. Suddenly, they realized that it was Allen! They all jumped up and moved in close to him. All three spoke at the same time.

"Allen!"

"Oh my, God!"

"My baby! Are you okay?"

"What happened? Where am I?" He asked groggily.

"You're in the hospital, son. How are you feeling?" Randall asked.

"I'm thirsty. Can I have some water?"

"Riann, go get the doctor!" Randall commanded. Without hesitation, Riann hurried out the door to get someone.

"How did I get here?" He asked, still trying to gather his senses.

"What do you remember?" Allyssa asked him first. Allen rested his head back on his pillow and thought for a moment.

"I remember being at the mall, hating the sound of Christmas music." He paused for a moment trying to regain the last things he remembered. Riann and the doctor came in at that moment and interrupted him.

"Hey, there young man. I'm Dr. Ramsey. Can you tell me who you are?" He asked while he used a flashlight to look into Allen's eyes and test his reflexes. Allen proceeded to answer his questions while the doctor continued his general examination.

"Excellent! Do you know why you're here today?"

"That's what I was just trying to tell my folks. I remember being at the mall shopping and having lunch with my sister."

"Okay. Very good. Anything else you remember?" They all looked at him, anticipating what his answer would be.

"Just that I was upset and irritated, which doesn't make sense because I love the holidays." Everyone was staring at him, which was making him slightly uncomfortable. He shifted his position in his bed and felt a pain in his back which made him flinch.

"Ouch!" Everyone reached out to him, and they all spoke simultaneously telling him to relax, and take it easy. Allen was getting frustrated and told everyone to back off. "Can someone tell me what happened? How did I get here?"

"There was an incident yesterday with mall security. Do you remember anything about that?" The doctor asked gently, trying not to put too much pressure on him. Allen closed his eyes. Partly to try to recall what happened, but mostly to block out the stares from everyone in the room.

"It's sort of like a dream. Really fuzzy." He squeezed his eyes tightly, trying to recall his memories.

"It's okay, son. Relax. Take deep breaths and take your time." Allen could hear Randall coaching him through like he always had when he was going through painful training exercises when he was growing up. Allen kept his eyes closed, as bits and pieces of the rest of memory over the last couple of days were coming back.

Tears formed in the corners of his eyes. Partly from the physical pain that he was feeling, but mostly the emotional pain of his family breaking up, and the trauma of almost dying. He began to hyperventilate,

181

and Dr. Ramsey sat on the edge of the bed, gently holding Allen at the shoulders, trying to calm him down. At first, Allen struggled to focus, but then he saw what appeared to be a brilliant light in the corner that was very soothing. Once he began to focus his attention on that, he could see the lady Angel that his parents had an encounter with.

She motioned with her hands for him to breathe in through his nose, and exhale through his mouth. As he followed her instructions, the room lit up brighter than before, but no one else seemed to notice. He could see their lips moving, but couldn't hear them speaking to him. Before long, the pain he had been feeling faded and the Angel did too. His vitals were stabilizing once again, and everything was returning to normal. Suddenly Allen felt more remarkable than he ever had and felt an uncontrollable urge to get up.

The Petersons' and Dr. Ramsey tried to get him to sit back, but Allen was determined to rise. Everyone was astonished to see him firmly plant his feet on the ground without pain or help! After taking several steps, Allen turned to face them all.

"I can't believe it!" Dr. Ramsey

exclaimed. A single tear fell from his eyes too, as he scrambled to gather his tools to examine Allen again. Once the doctor was done with his examination, he was stunned. He could barely find the words to speak, but somehow managed to laugh with glee and amazement.

"Ha! As I live and breathe, this is truly a miracle folks! When I was examining Allen the first time, he wasn't wiggling his feet! I was afraid that he wasn't going to be able to walk. When I was looking in his eyes with my flashlight, his responses were there but they were slow. I don't know what happened within a matter of minutes, but he's completely healed! I mean, I want to keep him here in the hospital a couple of more days just to be sure, but it looks like he's going to make a full recovery!"

Everyone gathered around Allen and embraced him. Allyssa and Riann wiped tears of joy from their faces and laughed. Even though he didn't need their help, they walked him back to his bed where they all sat down. Randall came and stood in front of him and gave him a look over himself. If he hadn't been there to see it, he wouldn't have believed it either.

"Son, we prayed so hard for this. God

truly answered all of our prayers! Oh my! I have to stop by at the chapel and give a praise report to the lady that prayed with me yesterday."

"Yeah, that's right!" Allyssa concurred. "She was phenomenal!" The doctor overheard their conversation and interjected.

"I'm sorry, to interrupt, but what lady in the chapel?" Dr. Ramsey asked sounding confused.

"Angel… was her name. I spoke to her too." Allyssa added.

"Last night?"

"Yes." They both said, wondering what the big deal was.

"That's impossible." The doctor said.

"Our chapel is under construction and has been closed off to the public, especially during this pandemic. Aside from that, the Chaplain, that is normally on duty called out for a family emergency of their own. There would have been no one here for you to talk to."

"Well, you're mistaken. Someone was here last night in the chapel and she asked me to pray with her. Only, I got to tell her all about my issues, and she prayed the most incredible prayer I've ever experienced. I mean, it was like an encounter with heaven itself!"

"Exactly!" Randall said getting excited. "I went there too... well, it's more like I was drawn there, and I told her that my family was in deep trouble and she prayed with me and gave me instructions with anointing oil. I felt foolish at first, but afterward, I've never felt better! It's like you said, she had this amazing peaceful presence and brightness about her."

"Wow! Mom and Dad! You literally just described what I just felt just now! I saw her!"

"Where?" Everyone asked.

"In here! That's how I was able to get better! She was over there in the corner helping me breathe, and then the whole room lit up with a brilliant white light. For a second, I thought she was going to take me to heaven with her!"

"Can you describe her?" Dr. Ramsey stepped closer looking intrigued. The Petersons' stammered a little trying to describe her. They found it strange that they couldn't give a definitive description, but only one that was very vague.

"She's about my height," Allyssa said.

"She had light brown hair." Allen was

trying to remember.

"Yeah, about shoulder length, but it kind of covered her face though. Now that I think about it, I didn't get a good look at her face." Randall said, looking perplexed.

"I don't believe this! It's happening again." Dr. Ramsey stated. He leaned back against a counter in the room.

"What is it, doctor?" Riann asked with genuine curiosity.

"Over the past few years, especially during Christmas, I've heard other patients' experiences with a praying woman, that no one can really describe. The one thing that they all have said was that she was bright, peaceful, calming, and sometimes brought healing. I never believed it myself, but if I hadn't witnessed your miraculous healing…" He trailed off. "Folks, sounds like we have a resident angel here at this hospital." He nodded his head as he was coming to terms with what he had just said. He thought he sounded crazy, but slowly came to the realization that there was no other explanation.

Allyssa thought about the conversation that she had with her. "People come here for prayer, and I'm always here for them."

"God bless you, Angel. You have been truly heaven sent."

"I get that all the time." Allyssa's mouth dropped and she looked up at the doctor.

"I think you're right! She said that people just call her Angel, and she's here all of the time."

"I really don't see how there's any other way to explain it." Riann said in agreement.

"Exactly! And she disappeared before I had a chance to ask her what she wanted prayer for." Allyssa thought further resting her mouth on her thumb and forefinger.

"Well, if she was an angel, I think I know what she would want prayer for." Allen said.

"What's that?" Randall asked. Allen hesitated for a moment before continuing.

"Peace on earth and good will towards men." Allen's eyes scanned the room, and everyone nodded in agreement. It was bittersweet that he had been healed, but the fact that the rest of the world was still so ugly towards each other saddened him. Dr. Ramsey got a page and excused himself from the room and wished everyone a Merry Christmas before heading out. Allen shrugged and said, "I'm not trying to sound ungrateful, because I'm definitely happy to be alive, but the only thing that would make this Christmas a better one is if my parents would stay together." His eyes sank with sorrow. The rest of the Petersons' smirked a little and then Randall and Allyssa joined hands and said together, "Well, son, about that…" They giggled before going into an explanation as to what happened. From a distance Angel watched the Petersons' come together again joyfully and gave God praise for answering prayers heard and unheard. She knew that the world had a long way to go, but she was prepared to serve one after the other. She glided down the hallway singing softly to herself,

"Someday at Christmas men won't be boys playing with bombs like kids play with toys. One warm December our hearts will see a world where men are free…"

The End.

LOVE DESTINATION

CHAPTER ONE

It was the beginning of the fall season, and LaShay was in her home cuddled on the couch as she sipped a warm drink while she talked on the phone to her friend Amanda. "Come down for Thanksgiving Shay, you'll enjoy yourself, I promise you will not regret it," Amanda said.

"I don't know," LaShay hesitantly said.

"Oh, come on. What do you have to lose? I'm having several friends over for the holiday like last year.
When I told you how it went you thought it was a success, so what's stopping you?" Can you get the time off?"

"As a matter of fact, I can get off," stated LaShay. I'm just hesitant because I won't know anyone, but you and you'll be too busy being booed up with your man Brice."

"Look, there will be other single people, and it's not like we're trying to play matchmaker. The idea is for everyone to enjoy themselves," stated Amanda. "I have no control when cupid might surface, so if cupid shows up, it's not my fault!" Amanda said loudly, then chuckled which sent LaShay into the giggles. "Speaking of Brice, he'll be at his place most of the time, so it's not like I won't have time for my friends, and he will be spending time with his friends as well," Amanda explained.

"I can't say I'm not looking forward to seeing the single guys, said LaShay. What do they look like?"

" Uh, if I say so myself," Amanda paused and held the phone just to annoy LaShay.

"Hello, hello?"

"I'm here girl," Amanda laughed.

"Well!" LaShay said, annoyed, "Are they good-looking?"

"Yes!"

"Ok, ok, I am all in, and besides, I keep saying I want to start taking weekend trips," said LaShay.

"Right!" Amanda said sarcastically. LaShay went on to say, "Well, you could've saved your breath if you would've called and just said, girl, you need to get up here for Thanksgiving, Brice fine ass single friends will be here! Simple as that. That would have been all wrapped up neatly with a bow on top."

"Whatever," said Amanda, and rolled her

eyes playfully. "You are a hot mess."

"I'm so excited to get away, and it's nice to know eye candy is on the horizon."

"Girl, shut up with your crazy self. Speaking of weekend trips, I hope you enjoy yourself enough to return for Christmas."

"Amanda, put me down for Christmas if there is more eye candy, hello, ok?" They both giggled.

After filling up her tank, LaShay headed inside the gas station. She located the restroom sign and headed in that direction. Donovan stood in the gas station line and stretched with his fingers interlocked in front of him. He extended his arms above his head and took in a deep breath with his eyes closed. As he did, he took a deep breath and inhaled the sweet smell of cinnamon rolls and coffee mixed with perfume. His eyes instantly peered around to see who was wearing that amazing scent. He barely caught a glimpse of her backside as she headed towards the restroom.

After she exited the restroom, LaShay slowly looked through the store on her way towards the door. She didn't see anything that caught her eye that she wanted. Well, the one thing that was not for sale was the good-looking man at the counter who was turning around to see what pump his vehicle was at so he could tell the cashier which pump. They locked eyes for a second or two, and LaShay continued out the door to her car.

Donovan noticed what the lady was wearing and knew she must be the one who was wearing the enticing fragrance he smelled earlier. She's not bad looking either, Donovan thought as he tried to focus on which pump he was at as he watched the mystery woman's sexy hips sway as she walked. "Sir, how much and on which pump?" The gas station attendant asked Donovan. "Oh, I am sorry. I'm at pump five. Can you put forty dollars on it," Donovan replied? He quickly paid for the gas and headed out of the gas station.

CHAPTER TWO

Donovan was headed to Tennessee from Indiana to meet friends for Thanksgiving. As Donovan got back on the highway, he thought about the woman he locked eyes with. He wished he had gotten to speak with her. He thought, the next time I'm going to be more proactive. Man, I sure wanted to kiss her berry-colored lips. He played out in his mind what he was going to do the next time he was in that situation. Just as he was thinking about her, his phone rang.

"Hey Dewayne, are you on the road now?" Donovan asked excitedly.
"Yeah, I am. I wasn't expecting you to sound so happy about it though," Dewayne said curiously.

"Awe, man, I just saw this cutie, and duh, I think I'm still geeked up about it," Donovan replied."

"You must have gotten her number as excited as you sound," Dewayne responded.
Donovan sighed and replied, "No, I didn't, but I was just thinking about her when you called."

"She must have been a very striking

woman to consume your thoughts this way," Dewayne commented.

"Yeah, Dewayne, she was, and seeing her just made me feel like I'm ready to get back in the game!" Donovan said sincerely.

"I feel you man, jump on back out there," Dewayne said encouragingly.

"Well, she probably doesn't live anywhere near me, so it doesn't matter," Donavan said.

"Well, that could be true, but if I see someone, I'm interested in I'm going full throttle. I'm going to have the answers to all those questions, bet," Dewayne replied with full confidence.

"Hey, I need to take this call. I'll see you at Brice's soon, stay safe," Dewayne said before hanging up.

"Thanks, see ya," said Donavan.

Amanda and LaShay were so happy to see each other. Amanda gave LaShay a tour of her three-bedroom Townhome, and showed her where she would be sleeping.
LaShay got settled in and freshened up and went to the living room where she heard Amanda on the phone.

"Ok, see you shortly," Amanda said before hanging up the phone.

"So how many people will be joining us for the holiday, and what do you have planned?" LaShay asked.

"Well, there will be about 10 of us, two couples and six singles, Amanda replied.

"That was Yolanda and Michelle, and they will be here soon they are riding together. "Would you like some hot chocolate?" Amanda asked LaShay.

Sarcastically but playful, LaShay answered, "Yes, I would like my hot chocolate tall, dark and handsome in a mug with marshmallows to lay my head on for pillow talk."

"Girl, you are so silly," Amanda replied as she prepared the hot chocolate for LaShay.

Brice inherited his parent's 4 bedroom home when they moved to Florida, and he loved it, and he loved to entertain there. He heard a car door shut and went to the front door, and peered out to see it was Marcus getting out of his car. He opened the door and stepped out onto the porch. Marcus got out of his vehicle and headed up the walkway. They greeted each other, and Brice complimented Marcus on his new ride as they went inside.

Phillip and Charles were already been inside. They were putting supplies out for the care packages. They all greeted each other, and Brice told them to check out Marcus's new whip when they got a chance.

"I can't truly check it out without the keys and a sexy honey in the passenger seat!" exclaimed Scott.

"Right, right!" Phillip replied. They laughed and high five. Brice started to walk towards the stairs, "Follow me and I'll show you where you can put your things. If you're hungry, there is a pot of chili on the stove in the kitchen, just help yourself," Brice told Marcus.

"Yes, I'm ready to feast on something. I'll be right back down," Marcus quickly replied.

When they got to the room, they heard car doors shutting and voices coming from outside. They looked out the window and saw that Dewayne and Donovan had arrived. Phillip made his way out to greet them. "I'm glad you made it," Phillip said as he walked down the porch steps.

"Thanks, man," said Dewayne, and they did their side hug and backslap.

"Don, my man," Phillip greeted Donovan, and they hand pound.

"Whose ride is this?" Dewayne asked, pointing at the Jeep Wrangler in the driveway.

"Oh, that's Marcus's new whip. He is upstairs," Scott said as he came outside.
Scott pointed towards the upstairs window. Marcus tapped on the window and waved. They all checked out the new ride. Marcus yelled out the window, "DON'T TOUCH IT!" Dewayne reached inside his car and gave them hand sanitizer and they put it on and left their handprints on Marcus's vehicle windows. Marcus saw them, and he knew running out there was useless.

CHAPTER THREE

Back at Amanda's, Michelle and Yolanda had arrived and had settled in. They were in the living room chatting.

"Thanks for the cocoa. I love warm drinks," Michelle said in between sips.

"Yes, I agree," Yolanda chimed in.

"So, it's been a long time since we've all been together, I hope the ride wasn't bad," Amanda said.

"No, not at all," Michelle said.

"I guess not you were passed out the first few hours of the way it was like riding with a St. Bernard sitting next to me slobbering. Look, I got a picture right here!" Yolanda said.

They all laughed as Michelle tried to see if there was a picture of her on Yolanda's phone, but it was hard for Michelle to see because Yolanda was a good two feet taller and was waving her phone around. Michelle gave up and rolled her eyes playfully at Yolanda and said, "If you dare post that pic, you're gonna get it!"

"How was your drive, LaShay?" asked Amanda.

"It was nice and relaxing, but nothing exciting until I stopped to get gas and locked eyes with this handsome guy." Lashay replied.

She stared off for a second or two, and then she jarred back into reality at the sound of her friend's voice.

"Well, did he ask you for your number?" Michelle asked all wide-eyed.

"No, I was leaving, and he was in line. I didn't wait around."

"Well, the way you were looking off into space I'm surprised you didn't wait and ask him for his number,"

Michelle replied.

"Ok, I saw it too," said Amanda.

"Me three," said Yolanda.

"He's probably taken, and besides, there is no telling where he lives anyway." LaShay said.

"Enough of that, when are we going to see these cute friends of your Boo Brice?" asked LaShay.

"Yeah, some eye candy would be nice," Michelle chimed in. The ladies giggled like teenage schoolgirls.

"We can head on over there now. I'm sure it will be fine. We have care packages for the homeless to assemble while we get to know each other. We will eat pizza tonight and play some games, and maybe watch a movie."

Donovan put his things away and was daydreaming about the woman he didn't approach when he had the chance. He thought about his conversation with Dewayne and how he was right. I should have said something to her. Then he would know if she lived near or not. His last relationship ended up being a long-distance one, and it didn't go very well. He was left heartbroken, so the possibility of doing that again right behind the last one would definitely have to be with the right woman, he thought if he ever did that again.

The ladies arrived at Brice's home. It was very nice and cozy, with Fall decorations that greeted you from the front door.
Brice stood at the door and greeted them.
    "Hello, ladies! Welcome, and please make yourselves comfortable. You can place your coats on the coat rack, and if you like, you can take your shoes off and place them on the shoe rack. Hey, beautiful he turned to Amanda and kissed her.

Amanda turned to LaShay, "Brice, this is LaShay."

"I'm glad you decided to join us."

"You remember Michelle and Yolanda?" Amanda said as Brice shook their hand.

"Yes, I do, glad you could make it again. I'm glad you all had a safe trip. Come on in and join the rest of us. Amanda and I'll introduce you LaShay to everyone, although most of you know each other from before."
Brice did the introductions when Donovan looked across the room and stood in amazement. There she stood. The woman from the gas station! Was he dreaming, he thought? LaShay, this is Phillip and Charles. They will not be attending Thanksgiving dinner with us, but they will help us feed the homeless tomorrow. This is Marcus. You will see him for dinner tomorrow, "Dewayne this is LaShay," Brice said as he was interrupted by the doorbell.

"Excuse me, you guys can get started on the care packages and I'll be right back."
Brice came back to the dining room area, "Donovan, the door, it's for you." LaShay looked up, and again she locked eyes with the man from the gas station, "So that's his name. What's he doing here?" She thought as her heart started pounding.

Dewayne was getting the assembling of the care packages going and assigned each person something to do. He was paying a lot of attention to LaShay and was chatting with her and getting to know her.

Amanda walked over to them. "Dewayne, will you and LaShay get the rest of the care package supplies out of my trunk since you both have your shoes on?" They both agreed and went to get their coats and headed outside to Amanda's car.

Donovan was outside with a female and it didn't look like he was happy to see her. They heard him say the word no and threw his hands up in the air to emphasize the meaning of the word. Dewayne looked and saw who Donovan was talking to and commented under his breath, "What is she doing here?"

Then he nodded his head in agreement when it looked like Donovan stood his ground, "Good for him." Dewayne finished getting the supplies. Donovan looked in their direction when LaShay closed the trunk of the car. He saw them head back inside.

Dewayne carried a couple of boxes. "Oh no," Donovan thought. He didn't want LaShay to see him like this and get the wrong idea. He didn't want to ruin a chance with getting to know her.

Donovan turned his attention back to his ex-girlfriend Shona.

"I don't know why you thought it would be a good idea to drop in at my friend's house just because I was in town." It's over between us.

"I thought it would be ok to hang out and make care packages. What harm is there in that?" Shona replied as she clutched the box of supplies.

"No, you don't have to do that here, you probably don't even care about the underprivileged you're only doing this to get to me."

You should be ashamed of yourself for coming over to Brice's home unannounced," Donovan said and he left Shona and went back inside.

CHAPTER FOUR

Once inside, LaShay walked up to Amanda to return her keys to her. She whispered to her, "Donovan is the guy from the gas station I told you about." Amanda's eyes got big, and she replied, "No way."

"Yes way," and he's outside conversing with a female in a heated discussion," LaShay replied.

"What Brice hasn't said one word, I bet it's his ex," Amanda said slowly in a shocked tone.

"Dewayne recognized her because he mumbled, what's she doing here?" LaShay commented.

Amanda's mouth hung open. She couldn't believe her ears. Did Shona show up attempting to beg Donovan back after their breakup she wondered?

Just then, Donovan returned inside. He stood at the end of the table next to Brice and started assembling care packages. "You good?" Brice asked.

"Yeah, she's gone. I'm sorry about that man, I had no idea she would do that," Donovan replied.

"No harm done," Brice said and patted Donovan on the back.

As they packed up the last care packages, the food delivery came, and they started putting it on the table. Brice walked over to Donovan, "Hey, I was just about to introduce you when the doorbell rang." He told Amanda to tap LaShay. LaShay turned around and walked around to the side of the table. As she came closer to Donovan, he smelled the same fragrance earlier in the gas station. Brice said, "LaShay this is Donovan."

Amanda stood by and smiled as she looked at them. Dewayne walked up and pulled the chair out for LaShay, she thanked him and sat down, and he sat next to her.

Donovan attempted to sit on the other side of LaShay, but Michelle glided in the seat next to Marcus, "Damn." Donovan mumbled under his breath.

Brice stood up and said, "I want to say a quick prayer, thank you, Lord, for this food that we are about to receive and for the safe travels of my guests that have traveled near and far, amen." Everyone said amen in unison, then he continued. "Well, let's go around the table and state where we're from.

Several people were from the same city, and that was no big deal. What shocked LaShay was when she heard Donovan say he was from Indianapolis.

"Oh, so is LaShay," said Amanda.

"Well, how nice. Shay, you have a travel buddy on the way back home, well, that's up to you guys," said Amanda.

"That's fine with me," replied Donovan, as he smiled at LaShay.

"Hey Donovan, hold up," Dewayne said as he and Donovan stepped away from everyone.

"I saw you talking to Shona, and I hope you're not considering taking her back after she tried to talk to me behind your back when you moved out of town."

"Not in a million years," Donovan said with a frown. Good looking out, you are a true friend."

"Donovan, you're like a brother to me," Dewayne replied.

With excitement in his voice, Donovan said, "That's her, LaShay is the lady from the gas station I wished I had a second chance to holler at!"

"What a coincidence," Dewayne replied.

"Oh, I see," Dewayne said in a slow and hesitant voice.

He nodded his head like he was thinking.

"What do you see?" asked Donovan.

"I'm just speculating," Dewayne went on to say, "but you probably were hesitant to speak to her under the situation because if you two hit it off. You probably didn't want to end up right back in a long-distance relationship again."

"You took some psychology classes, and you think you a shrink," Donovan said jokingly.

"I hate that she even saw that little blow up with Shona and me because no one wants to get involved with you if they think you bring baggage and drama," Donovan expressed to Dewayne.

"Look, you and Shona weren't yelling, but the conversation looked intense, and we only heard you say no if that makes you feel better," Dewayne replied.

While everyone was mixing and mingling, playing board games, and listening to music, Donovan looked around and saw LaShay was ending a card game with Phillip, Michelle, and Marcus. He approached the table and said, "So LaShay, what side of Indy are you from? I'm from the Castleton area?"

"I live in the Avon area," she replied.

"Where is that? I haven't lived in Indy long. I recently moved there from Kentucky," Donovan said.

"Oh, it's on the west side of Indy," LaShay replied.

"We're about to start another round of Tonk you want in Donovan? Phillip asked while he shuffled the cards.

"Yeah Casanova," Michelle said sarcastically. She laughed, and he shook his head as he reacted to Michelle. Michelle looked at Marcus and said, "Is that a smile?" Marcus tried to hide it, but he started to laugh and shook his head as he looked back and forth from Michelle to his cards. This got Michelle started.

"I'm breaking him down!

"What's she talking about?" asked Donovan.

"They have been playfully flirting all evening, and Marcus was playing hard to get," Phillip replied.

"Ha! Ha! Ha!" The whole table looked at Marcus and Michelle and burst into laughter.

Brice pulled Amanda into his arms and said, "If things go the way I think, we may have to call our holiday get-together this year

The Love Retreat, or The Love Destination Spot." Amanda laughed, and they kissed.

CHAPTER FIVE

When they arrived at Brice's home Thanksgiving morning for breakfast, the house smelled so amazing! Amanda had previously prepared a breakfast casserole with Brice, and he popped it in the oven with biscuits.

Brice popped the turkey in the oven when the casserole and biscuits came out.

That morning Cindy and Scott joined them. They were a sweet interracial couple. LaShay hadn't met many African American women who were in an interracial relationship, it didn't matter to her who you dated, and she wasn't against it or anything. It was becoming more of the norm, and she was happy to see more African American females exploring their options.

Donovan sat by LaShay, at breakfast where they both joked and laughed with others enjoying each other's company. It was a relaxing atmosphere getting to know everyone, especially Donovan.

Well, everyone, we can carpool over to the church while the turkey bakes in the oven. I got up early and prepared it, and I took a before picture before I popped it in the oven," Brice said as he proudly looked at the turkey.

"What is he talking about, isn't the turkey already done?" Scott asked.

"Yes, it's is. He's just pulling everyone's leg. They delivered the food earlier. It only needs to be heated up," Cindy replied.

With an Italian accent, Brice said, "I've always wanted to say let me take a before pic of my masterpiece." Several people spoke all at once, "Oh shut up!"

"I know right!"

Brice got hit with a dishtowel. Laughter filled the room. Brice's silliness and the other's reaction had tickled LaShay into laughter as well. Donovan looked over at LaShay and said, "You have a pretty smile."

"Thank you, and so do you in a manly way," LaShay said as she walked off to get her coat. Donovan's smile widened even more as he was left standing there.

Inside the church, Amanda and Brice placed the care packages in a certain area of the church. Then they checked in their team and were shown where they would work.

"Wow, this kitchen is like Grand Central Station," LaShay said.

"Yes, it is, and there are so many needy families and elderly," Donovan said.

"Come, we must get scrubbed in like for surgery," Yolanda said.

LaShay gave her a puzzled look, but followed her and the rest of her party. They washed their hands and put on hair bonnets and protective gloves, masks, and what looked like a thin paper gown. The looked like they were ready for surgery. They were put to work. LaShay fell right in line with the others and spent two hours fixing dinners, and boxing them up, etc.

LaShay admired how diligent Donovan worked during the time they were at the church volunteering.

"That was very enlightening. I didn't know that many people signed up for dinners," Lashay said to Donovan.

"Yes, there are many people in need."

"I'm pooped, and you look like you are full of energy!"

"I'm built that way Lil lady. If I knew you better, I'd offer to rub your feet, but maybe next year," Donovan said as he smiled.

"Next year?" LaShay asked.

"Yes, I hoped to see you next year same

time, same place," Donovan said.

"How will you get to know me better and rub my feet from now until then?" LaShay asked.

"Good question. Will you take my number so that after we go home, we can get to know each other better?" Donovan asked. Donovan smiled to himself because his lead in question worked as planned, and he was glad LaShay asked that question and was interested in return, and he wasn't left out on a limb looking stupid.

"Yes, what's your number?" LaShay asked. They both exchanged numbers.

Thanksgiving Dinner

Back at Brice's, everyone gathered around the table, and Brice asked everyone to hold hands and bow their head as he blessed the meal. After the meal, everyone helped clear away the table. They mingled for a while, played games, and some of the guys watched football for a while.
Amanda asked everyone to gather to share some future goals for the year.

"What is this about?" LaShay whispered to Yolanda?

"We take time to share our goals if you

want, what projects you're working on, things like that," Yolanda replied.

"Oh no, for some reason, when Amanda told me we were going to do this. I thought we were going to do this at her place while painting our toenails or something, not in front of them." Shay's voice cracked when she said, them.

The women laughed.

"I'm sorry for the misunderstanding," Amanda replied.

"Just know, everyone isn't in the same place in their lives, and may not have big fancy set goals, so no worries Shay, share what you want. Just chime in whenever you want. We all know this is your first time with all of us."

"Right, and they may feel the same way sharing in front of us, but we're friends.

LaShay was amazed at the things she heard from others and was touched. The phrase she often heard, don't judge a book by its cover, could be applied to this group of people in this room. Some of the goals that were shared were of starting an online business like a boutique or expanding items they were selling on Amazon. Someone else wrote a book and attended a writer's retreat. There were some goals like positioning

214

themselves to be able to apply for a higher-level position on their job when the next one becomes available. Some just said they were exploring different interests. LaShay admired that as friends, several of them said they were going to help support one of the others in their goal. That touched her spirit. When Donovan spoke, she was all ears.

"Even though my job relocated me to Indy, I'm going to continue to support the youth program I started in Louisville with Dewayne and my goal is for us to duplicate that in Indy but expand it to include a program that teaches self-defense."

Dewayne was much deeper than LaShay realized she learned that not only had he started a youth group, but yearly they all gave to the homeless shelter because of him, he had started giving and contributing his own money to making care packages and collecting supplies for the homeless. They saw how passionate he was about it and he asked them to help him put packets together one day and it took off from there. He does this in his hometown in Kentucky and he has gotten his friends involved in Tennessee, Illinois, Ohio, and Indiana. It's amazing the impact one person can have on many.

LaShay decided to go next. "Wow, I must say I'm impressed with the goals I've heard, and I do donate to the Domestic Violence Shelter and the homeless initiative programs as well, so it's good to know we have that in common. One goal I want to share is called Adopt a Grandparent. I was involved in a program like this as a child and I loved it. It's bridging a gap between the youth and senior citizens that may not have grandparents or grandchildren in their life. Even though I had grandparents some seniors didn't have grandchildren. The senior citizens I was involved with were in a nursing home. I've started this program in Indianapolis and with my friend Nikki in Ohio, and it's been going well. So, I'm hoping it catches on and I'm very open to ideas and it doesn't have to be just nursing home seniors."

After everyone went around and spoke, Dewayne approached LaShay.

"Hey, little lady I wanted to say I can definitely see that program being a benefit to the community and the youth. I want to converse further with you about that."

"Sounds good, I think that would be a great benefit to your program," replied LaShay.

216

"Here is my card with my number. We have so much in common call me, it would be nice to just chat sometimes I like your energy," Dewayne said as he passed LaShay his business card.

Looking at Dewayne's business card, LaShay replies, "Oh, so you are a musician too. I see you play the saxophone and piano! With your music talents have you thought about getting the youth involved in playing an instrument?" LaShay asked.

"It's funny you asked that, I didn't mention it when we were talking about our goals, but I have something in the works," Dewayne replied as he winked at her.

"Wow, I'm impressed you have a lot of positive things going on and are so talented." LaShay replied.

"Thank you, you are as well, when I was listening to you speak about your goals, I was impressed with the many talents you hold, you're an author with your third book about to drop, you play: the violin, flute, and guitar. I was thinking maybe we can come to each other's event sometimes" replied Dewayne.

"That would be great!" LaShay replied with a hint of excitement in her voice. She was thinking how refreshing to meet someone with like interests and similar goals. Donovan stood and observed LaShay and Dewayne and he didn't like how Dewayne was paying Lashay so much attention. He told him how much he wished for a second chance to see her and now that he had he wasn't going to pass it up. So why was Dewayne smiling all up in her face like that?

"Yo Dewayne," Donovan beckons Dewayne over to the fireplace area where he was stacking some firewood with Brice.

"Let me see what this buster wants," Dewayne said to LaShay as he walked off.

"What you call him for we got this?" Brice said to Donovan.

Dewayne strolled over and said, "What's up Don?"

Donovan stopped stacking the firewood and looked at Dewayne directly in the face and said, "That's what I want to know?"

"What are you talking about?" Dewayne looked at Donovan a bit confused.

Brice stood up and said to Dewayne, "LaShay dude, you know he sweet on her, and he in his feelings right now." Brice shook his head and looked at Donovan.

"Really Don?"

218

"Oh really, I wouldn't be all up in a girls face like he was if I knew he was interested in her," exclaimed Donovan.

"I can't believe him," Dewayne said as he looked at Brice, then he turned and looked at Donovan and said, "I wouldn't do that, but since you went there, may the best man win."

"Oh, he will," Donovan quickly replied.

"Yawl petty," replied Brice.

CHAPTER SIX

Later that evening in the family room. Everyone sat around eating again and some were playing games on the card table, while others sat near the fire. It was cozy and everyone was talking and socializing.

"LaShay, did you say your book that's coming out is a book of motivational quotes?" Dewayne asked,

"Yes, but there is a section that has humorous quotes as well."

"Let me know when the book signing is in Indianapolis, so I can be the first one in line there like I will be in Louisville." Dewayne chimed in.

"Oh, you're having a book signing?" Donovan asked.

"Yes, Dewayne suggested since I haven't before I should this time, and he is going to set it up at the youth center on Community Day so I can sign all the books for the kids at the youth center and get exposure." LaShay replied to Donovan.

"All the kids can't afford to purchase a book, so I'll help cover the cost, so you won't have to donate so many books,"

Donovan replied, assuming LaShay would be donating books to the youth.

"That's very sweet of you, but Dewayne already said he's buying all the kids at the Louisville youth center a copy," LaShay replied.

"They're not just going to get a free book to toss about, naw naw they'll have to recite a quote or something out of it when we come together and talk about something positive, they've learned or heard," Dewayne commented.

"That's what's up! Sounds like a plan to move forward at the Indy location right guys?" Brice asked.

"I got that location," said Donovan.

"Wow, looks like you have pre-orders already girl," Michelle chimed in.

"Yeah, a double shipment," Amanda said under her breath while looking at Brice. Brice blew Amanda a kiss and smiled at her as he gobbled down some sweet potato pie. Yolanda giggled at their interaction.

As the ladies were getting ready to leave Brice and Amanda were in the foyer as the car was warming up. LL Cool Jay's song was playing, and Amanda was singing, "the ladies love cool J, cool cool J."

"Not up through these parts it looks like

the lyrics are the ladies love Dewayne and Donovan", Brice said as they started laughing. He kissed Amanda then said, "Babe, we're gonna have to change the retreat name to a thin line between love and hate."

"Shut up you big Goober," Amanda said, as she laughed and hit him playfully.

On the ride to Amanda's.

"I was ready to go, but not ready to go, it was getting tense in there, I hope the guys will be ok," Amanda said.

"I sure hope so," said Yolanda.

"Mmmm hmm, I want to know how our girl LaShay is feeling getting double-teamed?" exclaimed Michelle.

"What are you talking about?" asked LaShay.

Amanda explained "For real, you didn't see how Dewayne and Donovan were falling all over you? Brice gave me the 411 on a little conversation the two of them had and they both seem to have a thing for you Shay."

"Everything was on the up and up with my conversation with Dewayne, he never said anything out the way," LaShay replied.

"If you had met Dewayne somewhere else and had some small talk and got to know him a bit, would you have given him your number? Amanda asked.

"Well, when put it like that, yes." LaShay replied.

"He probably feels the same way. Just tread lightly, ok. Amanda said in a cautious but caring way.

CHAPTER SEVEN

Three weeks later

LaShay and Donovan were at the Christmas Community Day at her book signing in Louisville, Kentucky. Dewayne had the kids that had arrived getting their book signed by LaShay and another teen taking their picture. Things were going well when Donovan saw Shona on the far end of the room with a box she was unloading at a table.

Donovan tapped Dewayne on the shoulder and beckons him away from the table where LaShay was signing books, and he said, "What is she doing here?" and he pointed in Shona's direction.

"She asked to be a part of the Community Event and I wasn't turning any vendors down, besides a part of her proceeds go towards care packages for the less fortunate, to our after-school snack program. I couldn't refuse her. She is a pretty good person," Dewayne said.

"If Shona is such a good person, then why don't you talk to her, instead of trying to get brownie points with LaShay," Donovan said angrily.

"Hmm, I just might do that." Dewayne quickly replied. He had no intention of acting on what he said, but he just wanted to get under Donovan's skin.

"Dude, you said she was no good yourself and warned me about her. Donovan replied.

"She sincerely apologized, and I listened to her. I didn't mention she seemed drunk.

"What!" Donovan replied.

"You know how I feel about that and what I went through as a kid being left alone for hours by my drunken parent. I just flipped out and called you and I'm sorry," Dewayne said.

"Did Shona try to come on to you when you tried to give her a ride home from the club that night or not?" Donovan asked.

"Yes, she did try to kiss me, and I got somebody else to take her home," explained Dewayne.

"Things may have been different had you told me this then," Donovan said as he walked off. All those times Shona tried to explain, and I wouldn't hear her out, I at least owe her an apology, Donovan thought.

"Look, let it go LaShay and others are

starting to look this way, we cool?" Dewayne asked.

"Yeah," Donovan replied.

"That looked like you two were in an intense conversation, LaShay said.

The last book LaShay signed was for a teen named Kalen who said, "I bet they were fussing over who could raise more money than the other for something. That's what they usually do Ms. LaShay they call it a friendly wager."

"They do, huh?" replied LaShay

"Yelp!" Kalen responded.

"Lil man gone somewhere," Dewayne said to Kalen.

"Yeah, go get you some business, Donovan chimed in too."

Kalen scurried off with Dewayne. LaShay and Donovan were alone at her event table.

LaShay turned toward Donavan and with a sly smile on her face and asked. "What were you really talking about with Dewayne, I saw Shona, was it about her perhaps?"

"I don't want to talk about it, it was nothing. You see, he and I are cool. I was just reminding him of his warning to me, about her and we agreed to disagree basically."

LaShay had a gut feeling there was more to it than what Donovan had admitted to.

"It's obvious he knew she would be here at the event he organized right, so why do you need to warn him about Shona at a community event? LaShay asked.

"It was nothing sweetie, but it does seem he's gotten to know her better than I thought. " Dewayne wanted to share some details that he didn't mention to me back when he told me she came on to him then that he wanted to get off his chest. It probably would've mattered then, but it's in the past." Donovan said.

LaShay found herself wondering why she was wanting to know how much better Dewayne and Shona were getting to know one another. She felt some type of strong energy for him. How could this be I like Donovan and Dewayne hasn't hinted he was interested, but Brice told Amanda otherwise. She directed her thoughts back to the conversation with Donovan.

"Oh, does that upset you if they are getting close?" LaShay asked."

"No, not like it would be if Shona and I had dated a long time and had been intimate, We dated about four months right before I moved away," Donovan replied. What got to

Donovan a bit was seeing how much Dewayne and LaShay had in common and Dewayne went out of his way to support her and she seemed to be eating out his damn hand. He knew how men operated. Before a man says it verbally, he will do things for a woman he cares about with good deeds and actions. Donovan turned his focus back to conversing with LaShay.

"You said he mentioned something that mattered in your breakup?" LaShay questioned Donovan.

"Dewayne felt it was important information he forgot to mention. Things turned out the way they were supposed to." Donovan responded.

"Why would he bring something up now that you are in another relationship? I thought we were cool. I didn't think he would try to break us up? LaShay asked.

"It wasn't like that," Donovan assured LaShay. I believe if it's meant to be it will be. I feel you and I are meant to be. Donovan leaned over and kissed LaShay.

"Oh is this the kissing booth because if it is let me get my money out!" asked a female voice.

"Sorry it's not," Donovan replied and they looked to where the voice came from and there stood Shona and Dewayne was walking upright behind her.

Dewayne said jokingly, "Yeah, if it's a kissing booth going on no one cleared that with me, but I think I should be first!"

Shona and Dewayne laughed at his joke. Donovan and LaShay gave a little laugh.

"Looking at you love birds, I think I need to get this book of positive affirmations. Maybe some of that will rub off on me," Shona said.

"Most definitely," Dewayne replied.

Dewayne introduced the ladies to one another and told them about Shona's contribution going towards helping the center and the underprivileged. Shona was very humble. He spoke of LaShay's talents and what an accomplished author she was. He even mentioned he signed up for the writer's group she's in and would like to do a book of poems maybe a few with her.

"Wow, I definitely would support you guys!" Shona said and she purchased a book from LaShay.

"Besides Dewayne, I've never met any other author before. This has to be exciting probably not like your first book signing!" Shona said to LaShay.

"This is my first book signing. Dewayne encouraged me to do it! I'm glad I did, but I didn't know you're an author Dewayne" LaShay replied."

"He's very humble and supportive like that to everyone and gives second chances to people too, even when others won't," Shona said as she glanced at Donovan.

Before going back to her table, Shona said. "Stop by my table for some gourmet popcorn and other homemade snacks you guys, and congratulations on your book."

"Thank you," LaShay replied."

"Ok." they all replied.

"I'll be back over so put me a sample set to the side," Dewayne said laughing.

CHAPTER EIGHT

Christmas Eve

Everyone was at Brice's home socializing. There wasn't anyone new this holiday. They were enjoying finger foods and making holiday cookies. They had care packages that they were going to put together like they did last holiday. There was a knock at the door and Brice went to answer it. Brice stepped back into the room with a box he sat by the care package supplies with a puzzled look on his face and said, "Dewayne that's for you."

"Oh, ok, that's probably my friend," Dewayne said as he headed to the foyer.

"Oh, we are having a new person join us," said Amanda.

Brice replied, "She's not new to you, other than LaShay everybody knows her it's not a new person, she came last year."

Brice made a face like a blowfish and his cheeks were full of air and he slowly let the air out of his mouth.

"Wheeeeeew" my boys are going to make me say, invitation-only Babe," Brice whispered to Amanda.

"Why…?" Amanda stopped her question

in midstream as Shona walked into the room with Dewayne.

"Everyone you know Shona! Shona everyone," Dewayne said.

If it weren't for the Christmas music playing you could've heard a pin drop.

"Hey girl," Michelle said and others chimed in right behind her and greeted Shona.

Tension was in the room. Shona greeted everyone and then she stopped in front of Donovan and LaShay.

Yolanda said, "Shona would you like some egg nog?"

"Hi Donovan. Hi LaShay, I didn't expect to see you so soon," Shona said to them, and then she turned to answer Yolanda, but before she could answer her, Michelle said, "Oh, you all know each other?"

"Yes, we were all at Dewayne's Christmas Community Day."

"Thanks for bringing the care package supplies, you know how we do," Dewayne said.

"No problem," Shona replied.

Donovan got up and beckoned Dewayne to chat out on the back porch.

"Man, what are you doing with Shona?" Donovan asked.

"Man, what's your problem, you're in a relationship, so why is this any of your concern? Dewayne replied.

"There is something called a code you know what I mean. Some stuff you don't do without getting clearance or some type of understanding." Donovan explained. LaShay positioned herself where she could peek at them out on the back porch. Even though she couldn't hear them and their backs were to the house, she could tell just from their body language it wasn't just a friendly chat. She looked around and others were not paying attention to them.

She felt indifferent because she felt they were talking about Dewayne showing up with Donovan's ex.

Later that evening on the ride back at Amanda's.

"I couldn't wait to get you alone. We need to catch up!" Amanda said to LaShay.

"Exactly," said Michelle

"Right," Yolanda chimed in.

"Ok, this is what happened." LaShay started.

"Hold on I got to call Cindy."Amanda interrupted.

"For real?" LaShay started chuckling.

Amanda called Cindy and got her on the car phone. LaShay filled them in on her book signing, and her suspension about Donovan and Dewayne's side chat's that they had at the community center and earlier that evening on the back porch, left her feeling like they both were holding something back.

"This is a twist, I thought it would be more of the guys going back and forth over you since Brice said Dewayne had a thing for you too," Amanda said.

"Yolanda added, I understand Dewayne hasn't come right out and said he's interested, but with all he's doing and saying he wants to write poems with you, I would've thought he was going for you until he showed up with Shona."

"Yeah, what's with those two?" asked Michelle.

" I wonder how serious those two are?"

"Call me crazy but I know I saw Dewayne starring at LaShay when he thought no one was looking."

"Noooo!" LaShay said in disbelief. You must be mistaken, it's not like that."

"Is it?" Amanda asked.

LaShay wanted to tell them she felt a little something for Dewayne, but she felt so

234

wrong. She felt it would go away. Why were her heartstrings being tugged at like this? She never thought she'd be in this type of situation.

CHAPTER NINE

Christmas Day

Everyone was up bright and early and off to the Church with the care packages.

At the church, LaShay looked around and caught Donovan and Shona chatting off to themselves.

"Wow, really dude, LaShay said out loud."

"Don't jump to conclusions," Amanda said after looking up in the direction Shay was starring and saw Donovan and Shona talking.

It didn't appear they were arguing, it looked like they were enjoying the conversation they were having. LaShay thought she would've felt better if they had been in a heated discussion instead.

When Amanda looked back in Donovan and Shona's direction they looked frozen in time and stared at each other. LaShay caught the sight of them too.

"Shay stop doing that!" Amanda said.

LaShay looked down. She had put several helpings of green beans in the to-go container while starring at Donovan and

Shona. That broke the stare between Donovan and Shona when they heard Amanda say Shay stop!" They looked in their direction.

LaShay stormed off towards the restroom and bumped right into Dewayne.

"What's wrong?" he asked.

"Nothing I'm just having a moment, I'll be ok, LaShay replied, as she pushed Dewayne to get past him, but he did budge.

"I can go get Amanda for you, or you can talk to me," Dewayne said to LaShay as he looked her in her eyes. "I'm a good listener."

"I feel stupid, I don't understand why I feel this way. I don't want to ruin anyone's holiday, but I think I want to go home. I don't feel Don is being truly truthful with me. The second he thinks I'm not looking he's off chatting it up with Shona. When I ask him about her he acts as though he can't stand her being around. I'm sorry I know she's your girlfriend, but the way they were just starring all up into each other's face like they were about to kiss or something." LaShay said to Dewayne.

"It's ok, she's not my girlfriend. We're cool and I thought why should she spend the holiday alone. She's hung out with the group

237

before, so I invited her. We became closer working for the church in our town, that's it." Dewayne said. I can talk to him and see where his head is at?

"I just want to go home, but I rode here with Donovan, LaShay said.

"I'll drive you and I don't want to hear another word. My aunt and uncle that live in Indy invited me over and now I'll take them up on their offer." Dewayne said.

"I appreciate it," LaShay said.

"We'll be there around 5 pm at the latest if we head out now, I'm glad the streets are clear and we don't have to worry about the ride," Dewayne said.

Amanda came around the corner to check on Shay, with Brice on her heels. As LaShay explained their plan to Amanda, Brice and Dewayne talked nearby.

"So how is Shona getting home, didn't you two ride together?" Brice asked Dewayne.

"Yeah, we did, I guess Donovan can drop her off in Lousiville on his way back to Indy," Dewayne replied. I'm just trying to help make the situation better.

"Part of this is your fault, I can't believe you two, and I hope you two can get past this. We've been like brothers," Brice said.

238

Brice walked over to Amanda and shook his head and looked at her and said, "I can't even begin to put a name on this holiday."

"I know Babe," Amanda replied.

New Year's Eve

Dewayne and Donovan did remain friends, as a matter of fact, they double-dated on New Year's Eve. They went on a romantic dinner train ride through the Kentucky mountains each with a beautiful beauty on their arm. They posted pictures to the rest of their friends. They were not surprised to see that they had different dates than at Christmas.

Happy New Year 2022 the picture caption read. Donovan was in the picture smiling from ear to ear. He looked into the shimmering eyes of none other than guess who, Shona. That wasn't as big of a surprise as Dewayne's date.

Dewayne was smiling with the lovely LaShay beside him in his arms enjoying the moment. It's ironic how Dewayne traveled from Kentucky to Indiana to see LaShay. Donovan did the same for Shona.

Happy New Year and what's your love destination?